"You might have lost, you know."

Amused by the lingering annoyance in Sydney's tone, Mikhail slid an arm around her waist. "I didn't."

"The point is that you arm wrestled for me as if I were a six-pack of beer."

His grin only widened. A six-pack would make him a little drunk, but that was nothing to what he'd felt when he looked up and saw the fascination in her eyes as she stared at his biceps.

"And then," she continued, making sure her voice was low, "you manhandled me."

"You liked it."

"I certainly—"

"Did," he finished for her, remembering the hot, helpless way she'd responded to the kiss. "So did I."

She would not smile. She would not admit for a moment to that spinning excitement she'd felt when he'd scooped her up like some sweaty barbarian carrying off the spoils of war. . . .

Dear Reader,

Welcome to Silhouette **Special Edition** . . . welcome to romance. Each month, Silhouette **Special Edition** publishes six novels with you in mind—stories of love and life, tales that you can identify with—romance with that little "something special" added in.

And may this December bring you all the warmth and joy of the holiday season. The holidays in Chicago form the perfect backdrop for Patricia McLinn's *Prelude to a Wedding,* the first book in her new duo, WEDDING DUET. Don't miss the festivities!

Rounding out December are more stories by some of your favorite authors: Victoria Pade, Gina Ferris, Mary Kirk and Sherryl Woods—who has written Joshua's story— *Joshua and the Cowgirl,* a spinoff from *My Dearest Cal* (SE #669).

As an extraspecial surprise, don't miss *Luring a Lady* by Nora Roberts. This warm, tender tale introduces us to Mikhail—a character you met in *Taming Natasha* (SE #583). Yes, Natasha's brother is here to win your heart—as well as the heart of the lovely Sydney Hayward!

In each Silhouette **Special Edition** novel, we're dedicated to bringing you the romances that you dream about—the types of stories that delight as well as bring a tear to the eye. And that's what Silhouette **Special Edition** is all about—special books by special authors for special readers!

I hope you enjoy this book and all of the stories to come.

Sincerely,

Tara Gavin
Senior Editor

NORA ROBERTS
Luring a Lady

Silhouette Special Edition

Published by Silhouette Books New York

America's Publisher of Contemporary Romance

To my nephew Kenni, my second-favorite carpenter

SILHOUETTE BOOKS
300 East 42nd St., New York, N.Y. 10017

LURING A LADY

ISBN: 0-373-09709-3

First Silhouette Books printing December 1991

Printed in the U.S.A.

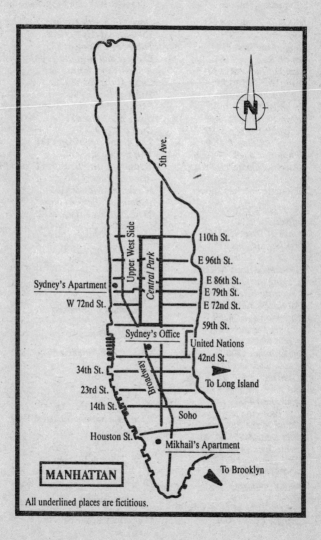

5th Ave.

110th St.
E 96th St.
Upper West Side
Central Park
E 86th St.
E 79th St.
Sydney's Apartment
E 72nd St.
W 72nd St.
59th St.
Sydney's Office
United Nations
42nd St.
34th St.
Broadway
23rd St.
14th St.
Soho
Houston St.
Mikhail's Apartment

To Long Island

To Brooklyn

MANHATTAN

All underlined places are fictitious.

Chapter One

She wasn't a patient woman. Delays and excuses were barely tolerated, and never tolerated well. Waiting— and she was waiting now—had her temper dropping degree by degree toward ice. With Sydney Hayward icy anger was a great deal more dangerous than boiling rage. One frigid glance, one frosty phrase could make the recipient quake. And she knew it.

Now she paced her new office, ten stories up in midtown Manhattan. She swept from corner to corner over the deep oatmeal-colored carpet. Everything was perfectly in place, papers, files, coordinated appointment and address books. Even her brass-and-ebony desk set was perfectly aligned, the pens and pencils marching in a straight row across the polished mahogany, the notepads carefully placed beside the phone.

Her appearance mirrored the meticulous precision and tasteful elegance of the office. Her crisp beige suit was all straight lines and starch, but didn't disguise the fact that there was a great pair of legs striding across the carpet. With it she wore a single strand of pearls, earrings to match and a slim gold watch, all very discreet and exclusive. As a Hayward, she'd been raised to be both.

Her dark auburn hair was swept off her neck and secured with a gold clip. The pale freckles that went with the hair were nearly invisible after a light dusting of powder. Sydney felt they made her look too young and too vulnerable. At twenty-eight she had a face that reflected her breeding. High, slashing cheekbones, the strong, slightly pointed chin, the small straight nose. An aristocratic face, it was pale as porcelain, with a softly shaped mouth she knew could sulk too easily, and large smoky-blue eyes that people often mistook for guileless.

Sydney glanced at her watch again, let out a little hiss of breath, then marched over to her desk. Before she could pick up the phone, her intercom buzzed.

"Yes."

"Ms. Hayward. There's a man here who insists on seeing the person in charge of the Soho project. And your four-o'clock appointment—"

"It's now four-fifteen," Sydney cut in, her voice low and smooth and final. "Send him in."

"Yes, ma'am, but he's not Mr. Howington."

So Howington had sent an underling. Annoyance hiked Sydney's chin up another fraction. "Send him in," she repeated, and flicked off the intercom with one frosted pink nail. So, they thought she'd be pacified with a junior executive. Sydney took a deep breath and prepared to kill the messenger.

It was years of training that prevented her mouth from dropping open when the man walked in. No, not walked, she corrected. Swaggered. Like a black-patched pirate over the rolling deck of a boarded ship.

She wished she'd had the foresight to have fired a warning shot over his bow.

Her initial shock had nothing to do with the fact that he was wildly handsome, though the adjective suited perfectly. A mane of thick, curling black hair flowed just beyond the nape of his neck, to be caught by a leather thong in a short ponytail that did nothing to detract from rampant masculinity. His face was rawboned and lean, with skin the color of an old gold coin. Hooded eyes were nearly as black as his hair. His full lips were shadowed by a day or two's growth of beard that gave him a rough and dangerous look.

Though he skimmed under six foot and was leanly built, he made her delicately furnished office resemble a doll's house.

What was worse was the fact that he wore work clothes. Dusty jeans and a sweaty T-shirt with a pair of scarred boots that left a trail of dirt across her pale carpet. They hadn't even bothered with the junior executive, she thought as her lips firmed, but had sent along a common laborer who hadn't had the sense to clean up before the interview.

"You're Hayward?" The insolence in the tone and the slight hint of a Slavic accent had her imagining him striding up to a camp fire with a whip tucked in his belt.

The misty romance of the image made her tone unnecessarily sharp. "Yes, and you're late."

His eyes narrowed fractionally as they studied each other across the desk. "Am I?"

"Yes. You might find it helpful to wear a watch. My time is valuable if yours is not. Mr...."

"Stanislaski," He hooked his thumbs in the belt loops of his jeans, shifting his weight easily, arrogantly onto one hip. "Sydney's a man's name."

She arched a brow. "Obviously you're mistaken."

He skimmed his gaze over her slowly, with as much interest as annoyance. She was pretty as a frosted cake, but he hadn't come straight and sweaty from a job to waste time with a female. "Obviously. I thought Hayward was an old man with a bald head and a white mustache."

"You're thinking of my grandfather."

"Ah, then it's your grandfather I want to see."

"That won't be possible, Mr. Stanislaski, as my grandfather's been dead for nearly two months."

The arrogance in his eyes turned quickly to compassion. "I'm sorry. It hurts to lose family."

She couldn't say why, of all the condolences she had received, these few words from a stranger touched her. "Yes, it does. Now, if you'll take a seat, we can get down to business."

Cold, hard and distant as the moon. Just as well, he thought. It would keep him from thinking of her in more personal ways—at least until he got what he wanted.

"I have sent your grandfather letters," he began as he settled into one of the trim Queen Anne chairs in front of the desk. "Perhaps the last were misplaced during the confusion of death."

An odd way to put it, Sydney thought, but apt. Her life had certainly been turned upside down in the past few months. "Correspondence should be addressed to me." She sat, folding her hands on the desk. "As you know Hayward Enterprises is considering several firms—"

"For what?"

She struggled to shrug off the irritation of being interrupted. "I beg your pardon?"

"For what are you considering several firms?"

If she had been alone, she would have sighed and shut her eyes. Instead, she drummed her fingers on the desk. "What position do you hold, Mr. Stanislaski?"

"Position?"

"Yes, yes, what is it you do?"

The impatience in her voice made him grin. His teeth were very white, and not quite straight. "You mean, what is it I do? I work with wood."

"You're a carpenter?"

"Sometimes."

"Sometimes," she repeated, and sat back. Behind her, buildings punched into a hard blue sky. "Perhaps you can tell me why Howington Construction sent a sometimes carpenter to represent them in this interview."

The room smelled of lemon and rosemary and only reminded him that he was hot, thirsty and as impatient as she. "I could—if they had sent me."

It took her a moment to realize he wasn't being deliberately obtuse. "You're not from Howington?"

"No. I'm Mikhail Stanislaski, and I live in one of your buildings." He propped a dirty boot on a dusty knee. "If you're thinking of hiring Howington, I would think again. I once worked for them, but they cut too many corners."

"Excuse me." Sydney gave the intercom a sharp jab. "Janine, did Mr. Stanislaski tell you he represented Howington?"

"Oh, no, ma'am. He just asked to see you. Howington called about ten minutes ago to reschedule. If you—"

"Never mind." Sitting back again, she studied the man who was grinning at her. "Apparently I've been laboring under a misconception."

"If you mean you made a mistake, yes. I'm here to talk to you about your apartment building in Soho."

She wanted, badly, to drag her hands through her hair. "You're here with a tenant complaint."

"I'm here with many tenants' complaints," he corrected.

"You should be aware that there's a certain procedure one follows in this kind of matter."

He lifted one black brow. "You own the building, yes?"

"Yes, but—"

"Then it's your responsibility."

She stiffened. "I'm perfectly aware of my responsibilities, Mr. Stanislaski. And now..."

He rose as she did, and didn't budge an inch. "Your grandfather made promises. To honor him, you must keep them."

"What I must do," she said in a frigid voice, "is run my business." And she was trying desperately to learn how. "You may tell the other tenants that Hayward is at the point of hiring a contractor as we're quite aware that many of our properties are in need of repair or renovation. The apartments in Soho will be dealt with in turn."

His expression didn't change at the dismissal, nor did the tone of his voice or the spread-legged, feet-planted stance. "We're tired of waiting for our turn. We want what was promised to us, now."

"If you'll send me a list of your demands—"

"We have."

She set her teeth. "Then I'll look over the files this evening."

"Files aren't people. You take the rent money every month, but you don't think of the people." He placed his hands on the desk and leaned forward. Sydney caught a wisp of sawdust and sweat that was uncomfortably appealing. "Have you seen the building, or the people who live in it?"

"I have reports," she began.

"Reports." He swore—it wasn't in a language she understood, but she was certain it was an oath. "You have your accountants and your lawyers, and you sit up here in your pretty office and look through papers." With one quick slash of the hand, he dismissed her office and herself. "But you know nothing. It's not you who's cold when the heat doesn't work, or who must climb five flights of stairs when the elevator is broken. You don't worry that the water won't get hot or that the wiring is too old to be safe."

No one spoke to her that way. No one. Her own temper was making her heart beat too fast. It made her forget that she was facing a very dangerous man.

"You're wrong. I'm very concerned about all of those things. And I intend to correct them as soon as possible."

His eyes flashed and narrowed, like a sword raised and turned on its edge. "This is a promise we've heard before."

"Now, it's my promise, and you haven't had that before."

"And we're supposed to trust you. You, who are too lazy or too afraid to even go see what she owns."

Her face went dead white, the only outward sign of fury. "I've had enough of your insults for one afternoon, Mr. Stanislaski. Now, you can either find your way out, or I'll call security to help you find it."

"I know my way," he said evenly. "I'll tell you this, Miss Sydney Hayward, you will begin to keep those promises within two days, or we'll go to the building commissioner, and the press."

Sydney waited until he had stalked out before she sat again. Slowly she took a sheet of stationery from the drawer then methodically tore it into shreds. She stared at the smudges his big wide-palmed hands had left on her glossy desk and chose and shredded another sheet. Calmer, she punched the intercom, "Janine, bring me everything you've got on the Soho project."

An hour later, Sydney pushed the files aside and made two calls. The first was to cancel her dinner plans for the evening. The second was to Lloyd Bingham, her grandfather's—now her—executive assistant.

"You just caught me," Lloyd told her as he walked into Sydney's office. "I was on my way out. What can I do for you?"

Sydney shot him a brief glance. He was a handsome, ambitious man who preferred Italian tailors and French food. Not yet forty, he was on his second divorce and liked to escort society women who were attracted to his smooth blond looks and polished manners. Sydney knew that he had worked hard and long to gain his position with Hayward and that he had taken over the reins during her grandfather's illness the past year.

She also knew that he resented her because she was sitting behind a desk he considered rightfully his.

"For starters, you can explain why nothing has been done about the Soho apartments."

"The unit in Soho?" Lloyd took a cigarette from a slim gold case. "It's on the agenda."

"It's been on the agenda for nearly eighteen months. The first letter in the file, signed by the tenants, was dated almost two years ago and lists twenty-seven specific complaints."

"And I believe you'll also see in the file that a number of them were addressed." He blew out a thin stream of smoke as he made himself comfortable on one of the chairs.

"A number of them," Sydney repeated. "Such as the furnace repairs. The tenants seemed to think a new furnace was required."

Lloyd made a vague gesture. "You're new to the game, Sydney. You'll find that tenants always want new, better and more."

"That may be. However, it hardly seems cost-effective to me to repair a thirty-year-old furnace and have it break down again two months later." She held up a finger before he could speak. "Broken railings in stairwells, peeling paint, an insufficient water heater, a defective elevator, cracked porcelain..." She glanced up. "I could go on, but it doesn't seem necessary. There's a memo here, from my grandfather to you, requesting that you take over the repairs and maintenance of this building."

"Which I did," Lloyd said stiffly. "You know very well that your grandfather's health turned this company upside down over the last year. That apartment complex is only one of several buildings he owned."

"You're absolutely right." Her voice was quiet but without warmth. "I also know that we have a responsibility, a legal and a moral responsibility to our tenants, whether the building is in Soho or on Central Park West." She closed the folder, linked her hands over it and, in that gesture, stated ownership. "I don't want to antagonize you, Lloyd, but I want you to understand that I've decided to handle this particular property myself."

"Why?"

She granted him a small smile. "I'm not entirely sure. Let's just say I want to get my feet wet, and I've decided to make this property my pet project. In the meantime, I'd like you to look over the reports on the construction firms, and give me your recommendations." She offered him another file. "I've included a list of the properties, in order of priority. We'll have a meeting Friday, ten o'clock, to finalize."

"All right." He tapped out his cigarette before he rose. "Sydney, I hope you won't take offense, but a woman who's spent most of her life traveling and buying clothes doesn't know much about business, or making a profit."

She did take offense, but she'd be damned if she'd show it. "Then I'd better learn, hadn't I? Good night, Lloyd."

Not until the door closed did she look down at her hands. They were shaking. He was right, absolutely right to point out her inadequacies. But he couldn't know how badly she needed to prove herself here, to make something out of what her grandfather had left her. Nor could he know how terrified she was that she would let down the family name. Again.

Before she could change her mind, she tucked the file into her briefcase and left the office. She walked down the wide pastel corridor with its tasteful watercolors and thriving ficus trees, through the thick glass doors that closed in her suite of offices. She took her private elevator down to the lobby, where she nodded to the guard before she walked outside.

The heat punched like a fist. Though it was only mid-June, New York was in the clutches of a vicious heat wave with temperatures and humidity spiraling gleefully. She had only to cross the sidewalk to be cocooned in the waiting car, sheltered from the dripping air and noise. After giving her driver the address, she settled back for the ride to Soho.

Traffic was miserable, snarling and edgy. But that would only give her more time to think. She wasn't certain what she was going to do when she got there.

Nor was she sure what she would do if she ran into Mikhail Stanislaski again.

He'd made quite an impression on her, Sydney mused. Exotic looks, hot eyes, a complete lack of courtesy. The worst part was the file had shown that he'd had a perfect right to be rude and impatient. He'd written letter after letter during the past year, only to be put off with half-baked promises.

Perhaps if her grandfather hadn't been so stubborn about keeping his illness out of the press. Sydney rubbed a finger over her temple and wished she'd taken a couple of aspirin before she'd left the office.

Whatever had happened before, she was in charge now. She intended to respect her inheritance and all the responsibilities that went with it. She closed her eyes and fell into a half doze as her driver fought his way downtown.

Inside his apartment, Mikhail carved a piece of cherrywood. He wasn't sure why he continued. His heart wasn't in it, but he felt it more productive to do something with his hands.

He kept thinking about the woman. Sydney. All ice and pride, he thought. One of the aristocrats it was in his blood to rebel against. Though he and his family had escaped to America when he had still been a child, there was no denying his heritage. His ancestors had been Gypsies in the Ukraine, hot-blooded, hot tempered and with little respect for structured authority.

Mikhail considered himself to be American—except when it suited him to be Russian.

Curls of wood fell on the table or the floor. Most of his cramped living space was taken up with his work—

blocks and slabs of wood, even an oak burl, knives, chisels, hammers, drills, calipers. There was a small lathe in the corner and jars that held brushes. The room smelled of linseed oil, sweat and sawdust.

Mikhail took a pull from the beer at his elbow and sat back to study the cherry. It wasn't ready, as yet, to let him see what was inside. He let his fingers roam over it, over the grain, into the grooves, while the sound of traffic and music and shouts rose up and through the open window at his back.

He had had enough success in the past two years that he could have moved into bigger and more modern dwellings. He liked it here, in this noisy neighborhood, with the bakery on the corner, the bazaarlike atmosphere on Canal, only a short walk away, the women who gossiped from their stoops in the morning, the men who sat there at night.

He didn't need wall-to-wall carpet or a sunken tub or a big stylish kitchen. All he wanted was a roof that didn't leak, a shower that offered hot water and a refrigerator that would keep the beer and cold cuts cold. At the moment, he didn't have any of those things. And Miss Sydney Hayward hadn't seen the last of him.

He glanced up at the three brisk knocks on his door, then grinned as his down-the-hall neighbor burst in. "What's the story?"

Keely O'Brian slammed the door, leaned dramatically against it, then did a quick jig. "I got the part." Letting out a whoop, she raced to the table to throw her arms around Mikhail's neck. "I got it." She gave him a loud, smacking kiss on one cheek. "I got it." Then the other.

"I told you you would." He reached back to ruffle her short cap of dusty blond hair. "Get a beer. We'll celebrate."

"Oh, Mik." She crossed to the tiny refrigerator on long, slim legs left stunningly revealed by a pair of neon green shorts. "I was so nervous before the audition I got the hiccups, then I drank a gallon of water and sloshed my way through the reading." She tossed the cap into the trash before toasting herself. "And I still got it. A movie of the week. I'll probably only get like sixth or seventh billing, but I don't get murdered till the third act." She took a sip, then let out a long, bloodcurdling scream. "That's what I have to do when the serial killer corners me in the alley. I really think my scream turned the tide."

"No doubt." As always, her quick, nervous speech amused him. She was twenty-three, with an appealing coltish body, lively green eyes and a heart as wide as the Grand Canyon. If Mikhail hadn't felt so much like her brother right from the beginning of their relationship, he would have long since attempted to talk her into bed.

Keely took a sip of beer. "Hey, do you want to order some Chinese or pizza or something? I've got a frozen pizza, but my oven is on the blink again."

The simple statement made his eyes flash and his lips purse. "I went today to see Hayward."

The bottle paused on the way to her lips. "In person? You mean like, face-to-face?"

"Yes." Mikhail set aside his carving tools, afraid he would gouge the wood.

Impressed, Keely walked over to sit on the windowsill. "Wow. So, what's he like?"

"He's dead."

She choked on the beer, watching him wide-eyed as she pounded on her chest. "Dead? You didn't..."

"Kill him?" This time Mikhail smiled. Another thing he enjoyed about Keely was her innate flare for the dramatic. "No, but I considered killing the new Hayward—his granddaughter."

"The new landlord's a woman? What's she like?"

"Very beautiful, very cold." He was frowning as he skimmed his fingertips over the wood grain. "She has red hair and white skin. Blue eyes like frost on a lake. When she speaks, icicles form."

Keely grimaced and sipped. "Rich people," she said, "can afford to be cold."

"I told her she has two days before I go to the building commissioner."

This time Keely smiled. As much as she admired Mikhail, she felt he was naive in a lot of ways. "Good luck. Maybe we should take Mrs. Bayford's idea about a rent strike. Of course, then we risk eviction, but...hey." She leaned out the open window. "You should see this car. It's like a Lincoln or something— with a driver. There's a woman getting out of the back." More fascinated than envious, she let out a long, appreciative breath. "*Harper's Bazaar*'s version of the executive woman." Grinning, she shot a glance over her shoulder. "I think your ice princess has come slumming."

Outside, Sydney studied the building. It was really quite lovely, she thought. Like an old woman who had maintained her dignity and a shadow of her youthful beauty. The red brick had faded to a soft pink, smudged here and there by soot and exhaust. The trimming paint was peeling and cracked, but that could be easily remedied. Taking out a legal pad, she began to take notes.

She was aware that the men sitting out on the stoop were watching her, but she ignored them. It was a noisy place, she noted. Most of the windows were open and there was a variety of sound—televisions, radios, babies crying, someone singing "The Desert Song" in a warbling soprano. There were useless little balconies crowded with potted flowers, bicycles, clothes drying in the still, hot air.

Shading her eyes, she let her gaze travel up. Most of the railings were badly rusted and many had spokes missing. She frowned, then spotted Mikhail, leaning out of a window on the top floor, nearly cheek to cheek with a stunning blonde. Since he was bare chested and the blonde was wearing the tiniest excuse for a tank top, Sydney imagined she'd interrupted them. She acknowledged him with a frigid nod, then went back to her notes.

When she started toward the entrance, the men shifted to make a path for her. The small lobby was dim and oppressively hot. On this level the windows were apparently painted shut. The old parquet floor was scarred and scraped, and there was a smell, a very definite smell, of mold. She studied the elevator dubiously. Someone had hand-lettered a sign above the button that read Abandon Hope Ye Who Enter Here.

Curious, Sydney punched the up button and listened to the grinding rattles and wheezes. On an impatient breath, she made more notes. It was deplorable, she thought. The unit should have been inspected, and Hayward should have been slapped with a citation. Well, she was Hayward now.

The doors squeaked open, and Mikhail stepped out.

"Did you come to look over your empire?" he asked her.

Very deliberately she finished her notes before she met his gaze. At least he had pulled on a shirt—if you could call it that. The thin white T-shirt was ripped at the sleeves and mangled at the hem.

"I believe I told you I'd look over the file. Once I did, I thought it best to inspect the building myself." She glanced at the elevator, then back at him. "You're either very brave or very stupid, Mr. Stanislaski."

"A realist," he corrected with a slow shrug. "What happens, happens."

"Perhaps. But I'd prefer that no one use this elevator until it's repaired or replaced."

He slipped his hands into his pockets. "And will it be?"

"Yes, as quickly as possible. I believe you mentioned in your letter that some of the stair railings were broken."

"I've replaced the worst of them."

Her brow lifted. "You?"

"There are children and old people in this building."

The simplicity of his answer made her ashamed. "I see. Since you've taken it on yourself to represent the tenants, perhaps you'd take me through and show me the worst of the problems."

As they started up the stairs, she noted that the railing was obviously new, an unstained line of wood that was sturdy under her hand. She made a note that it had been replaced by a tenant.

He knocked on apartment doors. People greeted him enthusiastically, her warily. There were smells of cooking—meals just finished, meals yet to be eaten. She was offered strudel, brownies, goulash, chicken wings. Some of the complaints were bitter, some were nervous. But Sydney saw for herself that Mikhail's letters hadn't exaggerated.

By the time they reached the third floor, the heat was making her dizzy. On the fourth, she refused the offer of spaghetti and meatballs—wondering how anyone could bear to cook in all this heat—and accepted a glass of water. Dutifully she noted down how the pipes rattled and thumped. When they reached the fifth floor, she was wishing desperately for a cool shower, a chilled glass of chardonnay and the blissful comfort of her air-conditioned apartment.

Mikhail noted that her face was glowing from the heat. On the last flight of stairs, she'd been puffing a bit, which pleased him. It wouldn't hurt the queen to see how her subjects lived. He wondered why she didn't at least peel off her suit jacket or loosen a couple of those prim buttons on her blouse.

He wasn't pleased with the thought that he would enjoy doing both of those things for her.

"I would think that some of these tenants would have window units." Sweat slithered nastily down her back. "Air-conditioning."

"The wiring won't handle it," he told her. "When people turn them on, it blows the fuses and we lose power. The hallways are the worst," he went on conversationally. "Airless. And up here is worst of all. Heat rises."

"So I've heard."

She was white as a sheet, he noted, and swore. "Take off your jacket."

"I beg your pardon?"

"You're stupid." He tugged the linen off her shoulders and began to pull her arms free.

The combination of heat and his rough, purposeful fingers had spots dancing in front of her eyes. "Stop it."

"Very stupid. This is not a boardroom."

His touch wasn't the least bit loverlike, but it was very disturbing. She batted at his hands the moment one of her arms was free. Ignoring her, Mikhail pushed her into his apartment.

"Mr. Stanislaski," she said, out of breath but not out of dignity. "I will not be pawed."

"I have doubts you've ever been pawed in your life, Your Highness. What man wants frostbite? Sit."

"I have no desire to—"

He simply shoved her into a chair, then glanced over where Keely stood in the kitchen, gaping. "Get her some water," he ordered.

Sydney caught her breath. A fan whirled beside the chair and cooled her skin. "You are the rudest, most ill-mannered, most insufferable man I've ever been forced to deal with."

He took the glass from Keely and was tempted to toss the contents into Sydney's beautiful face. Instead he shoved the glass into her hand. "Drink."

"Jeez, Mik, have a heart," Keely murmured. "She looks beat. You want a cold cloth?" Even as she offered, she couldn't help but admire the ivory silk blouse with its tiny pearl buttons.

"No, thank you. I'm fine."

"I'm Keely O'Brian, 502."

"Her oven doesn't work," Mikhail said. "And she gets no hot water. The roof leaks."

"Only when it rains." Keely tried to smile but got no response. "I guess I'll run along. Nice to meet you."

When they were alone, Sydney took slow sips of the tepid water. Mikhail hadn't complained about his own apartment, but she could see from where she sat that the linoleum on the kitchen floor was ripped, and the refrigerator was hopelessly small and out-of-date. She simply didn't have the energy to look at the rest.

His approach had been anything but tactful, still the bottom line was he was right and her company was wrong.

He sat on the edge of the kitchen counter and watched as color seeped slowly back into her cheeks. It relieved him. For a moment in the hall he'd been afraid she would faint. He already felt like a clod.

"Do you want food?" His voice was clipped and unfriendly. "You can have a sandwich."

She remembered that she was supposed to be dining at Le Cirque with the latest eligible bachelor her mother had chosen. "No, thank you. You don't think much of me, do you?"

He moved his shoulders in the way she now recognized as habit. "I think of you quite a bit."

She frowned and set the glass aside. The way he said it left a little too much to the imagination. "You said you were a carpenter?"

"I am sometimes a carpenter."

"You have a license?"

His eyes narrowed. "A contractor's license, yes. For remodeling, renovations."

"Then you'd have a list of other contractors you've worked with—electricians, plumbers, that sort of thing."

"Yes."

"Fine. Work up a bid on repairs, including the finish work, painting, tile, replacing fixtures, appliances. Have it on my desk in a week." She rose, picking up her crumpled jacket.

He stayed where he was as she folded the jacket over her arm, lifted her briefcase. "And then?"

She shot him a cool look. "And then, Mr. Stanislaski, I'm going to put my money where your mouth is. You're hired."

Chapter Two

"Mother, I really don't have time for this."

"Sydney, dear, one always has time for tea." So saying, Margerite Rothchild Hayward Kinsdale LaRue poured ginseng into a china cup. "I'm afraid you're taking this real estate business too seriously."

"Maybe because I'm in charge," Sydney muttered without looking up from the papers on her desk.

"I can't imagine what your grandfather was thinking of. But then, he always was an unusual man." She sighed a moment, remembering how fond she'd been of the old goat. "Come, darling, have some tea and one of these delightful little sandwiches. Even Madam Executive needs a spot of lunch."

Sydney gave in, hoping to move her mother along more quickly by being agreeable. "This is really very sweet of you. It's just that I'm pressed for time to-day."

"All this corporate nonsense," Margerite began as Sydney sat beside her. "I don't know why you bother. It would have been so simple to hire a manager or whatever." Margerite added a squirt of lemon to her cup before she sat back. "I realize it might be divert-ing for a while, but the thought of you with a career. Well, it seems so pointless."

"Does it?" Sydney murmured, struggling to keep the bitterness out of her voice. "I may surprise every-one and be good at it."

"Oh, I'm sure you'd be wonderful at whatever you do, darling." Her hand fluttered absently over Syd-ney's. The girl had been so little trouble as a child, she thought. Margerite really hadn't a clue how to deal with this sudden and—she was sure—temporary spot of rebellion. She tried placating. "And I was de-lighted when Grandfather Hayward left you all those nice buildings." She nibbled on a sandwich, a strik-ing woman who looked ten years younger than her fifty years, groomed and polished in a Chanel suit. "But to actually become involved in running things." Baffled, she patted her carefully tinted chestnut hair. "Well, one might think it's just a bit unfeminine. A man is easily put off by what he considers a high-powered woman."

Sydney gave her mother's newly bare ring finger a pointed look. "Not every woman's sole ambition centers around a man."

"Oh, don't be silly." With a gay little laugh, Mar-gerite patted her daughter's hand. "A husband isn't something a woman wants to be without for long. You mustn't be discouraged because you and Peter didn't work things out. First marriages are often just a testing ground.''

Reining in her feelings, Sydney set her cup down carefully. ''Is that what you consider your marriage to Father? A testing ground?''

''We both learned some valuable lessons from it, I'm sure.'' Confident and content, she beamed at her daughter. ''Now, dear, tell me about your evening with Channing. How was it?''

''Stifling.''

Margerite's mild blue eyes flickered with annoyance. ''Sydney, really.''

''You asked.'' To fortify herself, Sydney picked up her tea again. Why was it, she asked herself, that she perpetually felt inadequate around the woman who had given birth to her. ''I'm sorry, Mother, but we simply don't suit.''

''Nonsense. You're perfectly suited. Channing Warfield is an intelligent, successful man from a very fine family.''

''So was Peter.''

China clinked against china as Margerite set her cup in its saucer. ''Sydney, you must not compare every man you meet with Peter.''

''I don't.'' Taking a chance, she laid a hand on her mother's. There was a bond there, there had to be. Why did she always feel as though her fingers were just sliding away from it? ''Honestly, I don't compare Channing with anyone. The simple fact is, I find him stilted, boring and pretentious. It could be that I'd find any man the same just now. I'm not interested in men at this point of my life, Mother. I want to make something of myself.''

"Make something of yourself," Margerite repeated, more stunned than angry. "You're a Hayward. You don't need to make yourself anything else." She plucked up a napkin to dab at her lips. "For heaven's sake, Sydney, you've been divorced from Peter for four years. It's time you found a suitable husband. It's women who write the invitations," she reminded her daughter. "And they have a policy of excluding beautiful, unattached females. You have a place in society, Sydney. And a responsibility to your name."

The familiar clutching in her stomach had Sydney setting the tea aside. "So you've always told me."

Satisfied that Sydney would be reasonable, she smiled. "If Channing won't do, there are others. But I really think you shouldn't be so quick to dismiss him. If I were twenty years younger... well." She glanced at her watch and gave a little squeak. "Dear me, I'm going to be late for the hairdresser. I'll just run and powder my nose first."

When Margerite slipped into the adjoining bath, Sydney leaned her head back and closed her eyes. Where was she to put all these feelings of guilt and inadequacy? How could she explain herself to her mother when she couldn't explain herself to herself?

Rising, she went back to her desk. She couldn't convince Margerite that her unwillingness to become involved again had nothing to do with Peter when, in fact, it did. They had been friends, damn it. She and Peter had grown up with each other, had cared for each other. They simply hadn't been in love with each other. Family pressure had pushed them down the aisle while they'd been too young to realize the mistake. Then they had spent the best part of two years trying miserably to make the marriage work.

The pity of it wasn't the divorce, but the fact that when they had finally parted, they were no longer friends. If she couldn't make a go of it with someone she'd cared for, someone she'd had so much in common with, someone she'd liked so much, surely the lack was in her.

All she wanted to do now was to feel deserving of her grandfather's faith in her. She'd been offered a different kind of responsibility, a different kind of challenge. This time, she couldn't afford to fail.

Wearily she answered her intercom. "Yes, Janine."

"Mr. Stanislaski's here, Miss Hayward. He doesn't have an appointment, but he says he has some papers you wanted to see."

A full day early, she mused, and straightened her shoulders. "Send him in."

At least he'd shaved, she thought, though this time there were holes in his jeans. Closing the door, he took as long and as thorough a look at her. As if they were two boxers sizing up the competition from neutral corners.

She looked just as starched and prim as before, in one of her tidy business suits, this time in pale gray, with all those little silver buttons on her blouse done up to her smooth white throat. He glanced down at the tea tray with its delicate cups and tiny sandwiches. His lips curled.

"Interrupting your lunch, Hayward?"

"Not at all." She didn't bother to stand or smile but gestured him across the room. "Do you have the bid, Mr. Stanislaski?"

"Yes."

"You work fast."

He grinned. "Yes." He caught a scent—rather a clash of scents. Something very subtle and cool and another, florid and overly feminine. "You have company?"

Her brow arched. "Why do you ask?"

"There is perfume here that isn't yours." Then with a shrug, he handed her the papers he carried. "The first is what must be done, the second is what should be done."

"I see." She could feel the heat radiating off him. For some reason it felt comforting, life affirming. As if she'd stepped out of a dark cave into the sunlight. Sydney made certain her fingers didn't brush his as she took the papers. "You have estimates from the subcontractors?"

"They are there." While she glanced through his work, he lifted one of the neat triangles of bread, sniffed at it like a wolf. "What is this stuff in here?"

She barely looked up. "Watercress."

With a grunt, he dropped it back onto the plate. "Why would you eat it?"

She looked up again, and this time, she smiled. "Good question."

She shouldn't have done that, he thought as he shifted his hands to his pockets. When she smiled, she changed. Her eyes warmed, her lips softened, and beauty became approachable rather than aloof.

It made him forget he wasn't the least bit interested in her type of woman.

"Then I'll ask you another question."

Her lips pursed as she scanned the list. She liked what she saw. "You seem to be full of them today."

"Why do you wear colors like that? Dull ones, when you should be wearing vivid. Sapphire or emerald."

It was surprise that had her staring at him. As far as she could remember, no one had ever questioned her taste. In some circles, she was thought to be quite elegant. "Are you a carpenter or a fashion consultant, Mr. Stanislaski?"

His shoulders moved. "I'm a man. Is this tea?" He lifted the pot and sniffed at the contents while she continued to gape at him. "It's too hot for tea. You have something cold?"

Shaking her head, she pressed her intercom. "Janine, bring in something cold for Mr. Stanislaski, please." Because she had a nagging urge to get up and inspect herself in a mirror, she cleared her throat. "There's quite a line of demarcation between your must and your should list, Mr.—"

"Mikhail," he said easily. "It's because there are more things you should do than things you must. Like life."

"Now a philosopher," she muttered. "We'll start with the must, and perhaps incorporate some of the should. If we work quickly, we could have a contract by the end of the week."

His nod was slow, considering. "You, too, work fast."

"When necessary. Now first, I'd like you to explain to me why I should replace all the windows."

"Because they're single glazed and not efficient."

"Yes, but—"

"Sydney, dear, the lighting in there is just ghastly. Oh." Margerite stopped at the doorway. "I beg your pardon, I see you're in a meeting." She would have looked down her nose at Mikhail's worn jeans, but she had a difficult time getting past his face. "How do you do?" she said, pleased that he had risen at her entrance.

"You are Sydney's mother?" Mikhail asked before Sydney could shoo Margerite along.

"Why, yes." Margerite's smile was reserved. She didn't approve of her daughter being on a first-name basis in her relationships with the help. Particularly when that help wore stubby ponytails and dirty boots. "How did you know?"

"Real beauty matures well."

"Oh." Charmed, Margerite allowed her smile to warm fractionally. Her lashes fluttered in reflex. "How kind."

"Mother, I'm sorry, but Mr. Stanislaski and I have business to discuss."

"Of course, of course." Margerite walked over to kiss the air an inch from her daughter's cheek. "I'll just be running along. Now, dear, you won't forget we're to have lunch next week? And I wanted to remind you that...Stanislaski," she repeated, turning back to Mikhail. "I thought you looked familiar. Oh, my." Suddenly breathless, she laid a hand on her heart. "You're Mikhail Stanislaski?"

"Yes. Have we met?"

"No. Oh, no, we haven't, but I saw your photo in *Art/World*. I consider myself a patron." Face beaming, she skirted the desk and, under her daughter's astonished gaze, took his hands in hers. To Margerite, the ponytail was now artistic, the tattered jeans eccentric. "Your work, Mr. Stanislaski—magnificent. Truly magnificent. I bought two of your pieces from your last showing. I can't tell you what a pleasure this is."

"You flatter me."

"Not at all," Margerite insisted. "You're already being called one of the top artists of the nineties. And you've commissioned him." She turned to beam at her speechless daughter. "A brilliant move, darling."

"I—actually, I—"

"I'm delighted," Mikhail interrupted, "to be working with your daughter."

"It's wonderful." She gave his hands a final squeeze. "You must come to a little dinner party I'm having on Friday on Long Island. Please, don't tell me you're already engaged for the evening." She slanted a look from under her lashes. "I'll be devastated."

He was careful not to grin over her head at Sydney. "I could never be responsible for devastating a beautiful woman."

"Fabulous. Sydney will bring you. Eight o'clock. Now I must run." She patted her hair, shot an absent wave at Sydney and hurried out just as Janine brought in a soft drink.

Mikhail took the glass with thanks, then sat again. "So," he began, "you were asking about windows."

Sydney very carefully relaxed the hands that were balled into fists under her desk. "You said you were a carpenter."

"Sometimes I am." He took a long, cooling drink. "Sometimes I carve wood instead of hammering it."

If he had set out to make a fool of her—which she wasn't sure he hadn't—he could have succeeded no better. "I've spent the last two years in Europe," she told him, "so I'm a bit out of touch with the American art world."

"You don't have to apologize," he said, enjoying himself.

"I'm not apologizing." She had to force herself to speak calmly, to not stand up and rip his bid into tiny little pieces. "I'd like to know what kind of game you're playing, Stanislaski."

"You offered me work, on a job that has some value for me. I am accepting it."

"You lied to me."

"How?" He lifted one hand, palm up. "I have a contractor's license. I've made my living in construction since I was sixteen. What difference does it make to you if people now buy my sculpture?"

"None." She snatched up the bids again. He probably produced primitive, ugly pieces in any case, she thought. The man was too rough and unmannered to be an artist. All that mattered was that he could do the job she was hiring him to do.

But she hated being duped. To make him pay for it, she forced him to go over every detail of the bid, wasting over an hour of his time and hers.

"All right then." She pushed aside her own meticulous notes. "Your contract will be ready for signing on Friday."

"Good." He rose. "You can bring it when you pick me up. We should make it seven."

"Excuse me?"

"For dinner." He leaned forward. For a shocking moment, she thought he was actually going to kiss her. She went rigid as a spear, but he only rubbed the lapel of her suit between his thumb and forefinger. "You must wear something with color."

She pushed the chair back and stood. "I have no intention of taking you to my mother's home for dinner."

"You're afraid to be with me." He said so with no little amount of pride.

Her chin jutted out. "Certainly not."

"What else could it be?" With his eyes on hers, he strolled around the desk until they were face-to-face. "A woman like you could not be so ill-mannered without a reason."

The breath was backing up in her lungs. Sydney forced it out in one huff. "It's reason enough that I dislike you."

He only smiled and toyed with the pearls at her throat. "No. Aristocrats are predictable, Hayward. You would be taught to tolerate people you don't like. For them, you would be the most polite."

"Stop touching me."

"I'm putting color in your cheeks." He laughed and let the pearls slide out of his fingers. Her skin, he was sure, would be just as smooth, just as cool. "Come now, Sydney, what will you tell your charming mother when you go to her party without me? How will you explain that you refused to bring me?" He could see the war in her eyes, the one fought between pride and manners and temper, and laughed again. "Trapped by your breeding," he murmured. "This is not something I have to worry about myself."

"No doubt," she said between her teeth.

"Friday," he said, and infuriated her by flicking a finger down her cheek. "Seven o'clock."

"Mr. Stanislaski," she murmured when he reached the door. As he turned back, she offered her coolest smile. "Try to find something in your closet without holes in it."

She could hear him laughing at her as he walked down the hallway. If only, she thought as she dropped back into her chair. If only she hadn't been so well-bred, she could have released some of this venom by throwing breakables at the door.

She wore black quite deliberately. Under no circumstances did she want him to believe that she would fuss through her wardrobe, looking for something colorful because he'd suggested it. And she thought the simple tube of a dress was both businesslike, fashionable and appropriate.

On impulse, she had taken her hair down so that it fluffed out to skim her shoulders—only because she'd tired of wearing it pulled back. As always, she had debated her look for the evening carefully and was satisfied that she had achieved an aloof elegance.

She could hear the music blasting through his door before she knocked. It surprised her to hear the passionate strains of *Carmen*. She rapped harder, nearly gave in to the urge to shout over the aria, when the door swung open. Behind it was the blond knockout in a skimpy T-shirt and skimpier shorts.

"Hi." Keely crunched a piece of ice between her teeth and swallowed. "I was just borrowing an ice tray from Mik—my freezer's set on melt these days." She managed to smile and forced herself not to tug on her clothes. She felt like a peasant caught poaching by the royal princess. "I was just leaving." Before Sydney could speak, she dashed back inside to scoop up a tray of ice. "Mik, your date's here."

Sydney winced at the term *date* as the blond bullet streaked past her. "There's no need for you to rush off—"

"Three's a crowd," Keely told her on the run and, with a quick fleeting grin, kept going.

"Did you call me?" Mikhail came to the bedroom doorway. There was one, very small white towel anchored at his waist. He used another to rub at his wet, unruly hair. He stopped when he spotted Sydney. Something flickered in his eyes as he let his gaze roam down the long, cool lines of the dress. Then he smiled. "I'm late," he said simply.

She was grateful she'd managed not to let her mouth fall open. His body was all lean muscle, long bones and bronzed skin—skin that was gleaming with tiny drops of water that made her feel unbearably thirsty. The towel hung dangerously low on his hips. Dazed, she watched a drop of water slide down his chest, over his stomach and disappear beneath the terry cloth.

The temperature in the room, already steamy, rose several degrees.

"You're..." She knew she could speak coherently—in a minute. "We said seven."

"I was busy." He shrugged. The towel shifted. Sydney swallowed. "I won't be long. Fix a drink." A smile, wicked around the edges, tugged at his mouth. A man would have to be dead not to see her reaction—not to be pleased by it. "You look...hot, Sydney." He took a step forward, watching her eyes widen, watching her mouth tremble open. With his gaze on hers, he turned on a small portable fan. Steamy air stirred. "That will help," he said mildly.

She nodded. It was cooling, but it also brought the scent of his shower, of his skin into the room. Because she could see the knowledge and the amusement in his eyes, she got a grip on herself. "Your contracts." She set the folder down on a table. Mikhail barely glanced at them.

"I'll look and sign later."

"Fine. It would be best if you got dressed." She had to swallow another obstruction in her throat when he smiled at her. Her voice was edgy and annoyed. "We'll be late."

"A little. There's cold drink in the refrigerator," he added as he turned back to the bedroom. "Be at home."

Alone, she managed to take three normal breaths. Degree by degree she felt her system level. Any man who looked like that in a towel should be arrested, she thought, and turned to study the room.

She'd been too annoyed to take stock of it on her other visit. And too preoccupied, she admitted with a slight frown. A man like that had a way of keeping a woman preoccupied. Now she noted the hunks of wood, small and large, the tools, the jars stuffed with brushes. There was a long worktable beneath the living room window. She wandered toward it, seeing that a few of those hunks of wood were works in progress.

Shrugging, she ran a finger over a piece of cherry that was scarred with groves and gouges. Rude and primitive, just as she'd thought. It soothed her ruffled ego to be assured she'd been right about his lack of talent. Obviously a ruffian who'd made a momentary impression on the capricious art world.

Then she turned and saw the shelves.

They were crowded with his work. Long smooth columns of wood, beautifully shaped. A profile of a woman with long, flowing hair, a young child caught in gleeful laughter, lovers trapped endlessly in a first tentative kiss. She couldn't stop herself from touching, nor from feeling. His work ranged from the passionate to the charming, from the bold to the delicate.

Fascinated, she crouched down to get a closer look at the pieces on the lower shelves. Was it possible, she wondered, that a man with such rough manners, with such cocky arrogance possessed the wit, the sensitivity, the compassion to create such lovely things out of blocks of wood?

With a half laugh Sydney reached for a carving of a tiny kangaroo with a baby peeking out of her pouch. It felt as smooth and as delicate as glass. Even as she replaced it with a little sigh, she spotted the miniature figurine. Cinderella, she thought, charmed as she held it in her fingertips. The pretty fairy-tale heroine was still dressed for the ball, but one foot was bare as Mikhail had captured her in her dash before the clock struck twelve. For a moment, Sydney thought she could almost see tears in the painted eyes.

"You like?"

She jolted, then stood up quickly, still nestling the figurine in her hand. "Yes—I'm sorry."

"You don't have to be sorry for liking." Mikhail rested a hip, now more conservatively covered in wheat-colored slacks, on the worktable. His hair had been brushed back and now curled damply nearly to his shoulders.

Still flustered, she set the miniature back on the shelf. "I meant I should apologize for touching your work."

A smile tugged at his lips. It fascinated him that she could go from wide-eyed delight to frosty politeness in the blink of an eye. "Better to be touched than to sit apart, only to be admired. Don't you think?"

It was impossible to miss the implication in the tone of his voice, in the look in his eyes. "That would depend."

As she started by, he shifted, rose. His timing was perfect. She all but collided with him. "On what?"

She didn't flush or stiffen or retreat. She'd become accustomed to taking a stand. "On whether one chooses to be touched."

He grinned. "I thought we were talking about sculpture."

So, she thought on a careful breath, she'd walked into that one. "Yes, we were. Now, we really will be late. If you're ready, Mr. Stanislaski—"

"Mikhail." He lifted a hand casually to flick a finger at the sapphire drop at her ear. "It's easier." Before she could reply, his gaze came back and locked on hers. Trapped in that one long stare, she wasn't certain she could remember her own name. "You smell like an English garden at teatime," he murmured. "Very cool, very appealing. And just a little too formal."

It was too hot, she told herself. Much too hot and close. That was why she had difficulty breathing. It had nothing to do with him. Rather, she wouldn't allow it to have anything to do with him. "You're in my way."

"I know." And for reasons he wasn't entirely sure of, he intended to stay there. "You're used to brushing people aside."

"I don't see what that has to do with—"

"An observation," he interrupted, amusing himself by toying with the ends of her hair. The texture was as rich as the color, he decided, pleased she had left it free for the evening. "Artists observe. You'll find that some people don't brush aside as quickly as others." He heard her breath catch, ignored her defensive jerk as he cupped her chin in his hand. He'd been right about her skin—smooth as polished pearls. Patiently he turned her face from side to side. "Nearly perfect," he decided. "Nearly perfect is better than perfect."

"I beg your pardon?"

"Your eyes are too big, and your mouth is just a bit wider than it should be."

Insulted, she slapped his hand away. It embarrassed and infuriated her that she'd actually expected a compliment. "My eyes and mouth are none of your business."

"Very much mine," he corrected. "I'm doing your face."

When she frowned, a faint line etched between her brows. He liked it. "You're doing what?"

"Your face. In rosewood, I think. And with your hair down like this."

Again she pushed his hand away. "If you're asking me to model for you, I'm afraid I'm not interested."

"It doesn't matter whether you are. I am." He took her arm to lead her to the door.

"If you think I'm flattered—"

"Why should you be?" He opened the door, then stood just inside, studying her with apparent curiosity. "You were born with your face. You didn't earn it. If I said you sang well, or danced well, or kissed well, you could be flattered."

He eased her out, then closed the door. "Do you?" he asked, almost in afterthought.

Ruffled and irritated, she snapped back. "Do I what?"

"Kiss well?"

Her brows lifted. Haughty arches over frosty eyes. "The day you find out, you can be flattered." Rather pleased with the line, she started down the hall ahead of him.

His fingers barely touched her—she would have sworn it. But in the space of a heartbeat her back was to the wall and she was caged between his arms, with his hands planted on either side of her head. Both shock and a trembling river of fear came before she could even think to be insulted.

Knowing he was being obnoxious, enjoying it, he kept his lips a few scant inches from hers. He recognized the curling in his gut as desire. And by God, he could deal with that. And her. Their breath met and tangled, and he smiled. Hers had come out in a quick, surprised puff.

"I think," he said slowly, consideringly, "you have yet to learn how to kiss well. You have the mouth for it." His gaze lowered, lingered there. "But a man would have to be patient enough to warm that blood up first. A pity I'm not patient."

He was close enough to see her quick wince before her eyes went icy. "I think," she said, borrowing his tone, "that you probably kiss very well. But a woman would have to be tolerant enough to hack through your ego first. Fortunately, I'm not tolerant."

For a moment he stood where he was, close enough to swoop down and test both their theories. Then the smile worked over his face, curving his lips, brightening his eyes. Yes, he could deal with her. When he was ready.

"A man can learn patience, *milaya*, and seduce a woman to tolerance."

She pressed against the wall, but like a cat backed into a corner, she was ready to swipe and spit. He only stepped back and cupped a hand over her elbow.

"We should go now, yes?"

"Yes." Not at all sure if she was relieved or disappointed, she walked with him toward the stairs.

Chapter Three

Margerite had pulled out all the stops. She knew it was a coup to have a rising and mysterious artist such as Stanislaski at her dinner party. Like a general girding for battle, she had inspected the floral arrangements, the kitchens, the dining room and the terraces. Before she was done, the caterers were cursing her, but Margerite was satisfied.

She wasn't pleased when her daughter, along with her most important guest, was late.

Laughing and lilting, she swirled among her guests in a frothy gown of robin's-egg blue. There was a sprinkling of politicians, theater people and the idle rich. But the Ukrainian artist was her coup de grace, and she was fretting to show him off.

And, remembering that wild sexuality, she was fretting to flirt.

The moment she spotted him, Margerite swooped.

"Mr. Stanislaski, how marvelous!" After shooting her daughter a veiled censorious look, she beamed.

"Mikhail, please." Because he knew the game and played it at his will, Mikhail brought her hand to his lips and lingered over it. "You must forgive me for being late. I kept your daughter waiting."

"Oh." She fluttered, her hand resting lightly, possessively on his arm. "A smart woman will always wait for the right man."

"Then I'm forgiven."

"Absolutely." Her fingers gave his an intimate squeeze. "This time. Now, you must let me introduce you around, Mikhail." Linked with him, she glanced absently at her daughter. "Sydney, do mingle, darling."

Mikhail shot a quick, wicked grin over his shoulder as he let Margerite haul him away.

He made small talk easily, sliding into the upper crust of New York society as seamlessly as he slid into the working class in Soho or his parents' close-knit neighborhood in Brooklyn. They had no idea he might have preferred a beer with friends or coffee at his mother's kitchen table.

He sipped champagne, admired the house with its cool white walls and towering windows, and complimented Margerite on her art collection.

And all the while he chatted, sipped and smiled, he watched Sydney.

Odd, he thought. He would have said that the sprawling elegance of the Long Island enclave was the perfect setting for her. Her looks, her demeanor, reminded him of glistening shaved ice in a rare porcelain bowl. Yet she didn't quite fit. Oh, she smiled and worked the room as skillfully as her mother. Her simple black dress was as exclusive as any of the more colorful choices in the room. Her sapphires winked as brilliantly as any of the diamonds or emeralds.

But...it was her eyes, Mikhail realized. There wasn't laughter in them, but impatience. It was as though she were thinking—let's get this done and over with so I can get on to something important.

It made him smile. Remembering that he'd have the long drive back to Manhattan to tease her made the smile widen. It faded abruptly as he watched a tall blond man with football shoulders tucked into a silk dinner jacket kiss Sydney on the mouth.

Sydney smiled into a pair of light blue eyes under golden brows. "Hello, Channing."

"Hello, yourself." He offered a fresh glass of wine. "Where did Margerite find the wild horses?"

"I'm sorry?"

"To drag you out of that office." His smile dispensed charm like penny candy. Sydney couldn't help but respond.

"It wasn't quite that drastic. I have been busy."

"So you've told me." He approved of her in the sleek black dress in much the same way he would have approved of a tasteful accessory for his home. "You missed a wonderful play the other night. It looks like Sondheim's got another hit on his hands." Never doubting her acquiescence, he took her arm to lead her into dinner. "Tell me, darling, when are you going to stop playing the career woman and take a break? I'm going up to the Hamptons for the weekend, and I'd love your company."

Dutifully she forced her clamped teeth apart. There was no use resenting the fact he thought she was playing. Everyone did. "I'm afraid I can't get away just now." She took her seat beside him at the long glass table in the airy dining room. The drapes were thrown wide so that the garden seemed to spill inside with the pastel hues of early roses, late tulips and nodding columbine.

She wished the dinner had been alfresco so she could have sat among the blossoms and scented the sea air.

"I hope you don't mind a little advice."

Sydney nearly dropped her head into her hand. The chatter around them was convivial, glasses were clinking, and the first course of stuffed mushrooms was being served. She felt she'd just been clamped into a cell. "Of course not, Channing."

"You can run a business or let the business run you."

"Hmm." He had a habit of stating his advice in clichés. Sydney reminded herself she should be used to it.

"Take it from someone with more experience in these matters."

She fixed a smile on her face and let her mind wander.

"I hate to see you crushed under the heel of responsibility," he went on. "And after all, we know you're a novice in the dog-eat-dog world of real estate." Gold cuff links, monogrammed, winked as he laid a hand on hers. His eyes were sincere, his mouth quirked in that I'm-only-looking-out-for-you smile. "Naturally, your initial enthusiasm will push you to take on more than is good for you. I'm sure you agree."

Her mind flicked back. "Actually, Channing, I enjoy the work."

"For the moment," he said, his voice so patronizing she nearly stabbed him with her salad fork. "But when reality rushes in you may find yourself trampled under it. Delegate, Sydney. Hand the responsibilities over to those who understand them."

If her spine had been any straighter, it would have snapped her neck. "My grandfather entrusted Hayward to me."

"The elderly become sentimental. But I can't believe he expected you to take it all so seriously." His smooth, lightly tanned brow wrinkled briefly in what she understood was genuine if misguided concern. "Why, you've hardly attended a party in weeks. Everyone's talking about it."

"Are they?" She forced her lips to curve over her clenched teeth. If he offered one more shred of advice, she would have to upend the water goblet in his lap. "Channing, why don't you tell me about the play?"

At the other end of the table, tucked between Margerite and Mrs. Anthony Lowell of the Boston Lowells, Mikhail kept a weather eye on Sydney. He didn't like the way she had her head together with pretty boy. No, by God, he didn't. The man was always touching her. Her hand, her shoulder. Her soft, white, bare shoulder. And she was just smiling and nodding, as though his words were a fascination in themselves.

Apparently the ice queen didn't mind being pawed if the hands doing the pawing were as lily-white as her own.

Mikhail swore under his breath.

"I beg your pardon, Mikhail?"

With an effort, he turned his attention and a smile toward Margerite. "Nothing. The pheasant is excellent."

"Thank you. I wonder if I might ask what Sydney's commissioned you to sculpt."

He flicked a black look down the length of the table. "I'll be working on the project in Soho."

"Ah." Margerite hadn't a clue what Hayward might own in Soho. "Will it be an indoor or outdoor piece?"

"Both. Who is the man beside Sydney? I don't think I met him."

"Oh, that's Channing, Channing Warfield. The Warfields are old friends."

"Friends," he repeated, slightly mollified.

Conspiratorily Margerite leaned closer. "If I can confide, Wilhemina Warfield and I are hoping they'll make an announcement this summer. They're such a lovely couple, so suitable. And since Sydney's first marriage is well behind her—"

"First marriage?" He swooped down on that tidbit of information like a hawk on a dove. "Sydney was married before?"

"Yes, but I'm afraid she and Peter were too young and impetuous," she told him, conveniently overlooking the family pressure that had brought the marriage about. "Now, Sydney and Channing are mature, responsible people. We're looking forward to a spring wedding."

Mikhail picked up his wine. There was an odd and annoying scratching in his throat. "What does this Channing Warfield do?"

"Do?" The question baffled her. "Why, the Warfields are in banking, so I suppose Channing does whatever one does in banking. He's a devil on the polo field."

"Polo," Mikhail repeated with a scowl so dark Helena Lowell choked on her pheasant. Helpfully Mikhail gave her a sharp slap between the shoulder blades, then offered her her water goblet.

"You're, ah, Russian, aren't you, Mr. Stanislaski?" Helena asked. Images of cossacks danced in her head.

"I was born in the Ukraine."

"The Ukraine, yes. I believe I read something about your family escaping over the border when you were just a child."

"We escaped in a wagon, over the mountains into Hungary, then into Austria and finally settled in New York."

"A wagon." Margerite sighed into her wine. "How romantic."

Mikhail remembered the cold, the fear, the hunger. But he only shrugged. He doubted romance was always pretty, or comfortable.

Relieved that he looked approachable again, Helena Lowell began to ask him questions about art.

After an hour, he was glad to escape from the pretensions of the society matron's art school jargon. Guests were treated to violin music, breezy terraces and moon-kissed gardens. His hostess fluttered around him like a butterfly, lashes batting, laughter trilling.

Margerite's flirtations were patently obvious and didn't bother him. She was a pretty, vivacious woman currently between men. Though he had privately deduced she shared little with her daughter other than looks, he considered her harmless, even entertaining. So when she offered to show him the rooftop patio, he went along.

The wind off the sound was playful and fragrant. And it was blessedly quiet following the ceaseless after-dinner chatter. From the rail, Mikhail could see the water, the curve of beach, the serene elegance of other homes tucked behind walls and circling gardens.

And he could see Sydney as she strolled to the shadowy corner of the terrace below with her arm tucked through Channing's.

"My third husband built this house," Margerite was saying. "He's an architect. When we divorced, I had my choice between this house and the little villa in Nice. Naturally, with so many of my friends here, I chose this." With a sigh, she turned to face him, leaning prettily on the rail. "I must say, I love this spot. When I give house parties people are spread out on every level, so it's both cozy and private. Perhaps you'll join us some weekend this summer."

"Perhaps." The answer was absent as he stared down at Sydney. The moonlight made her hair gleam like polished mahogany.

Margerite shifted, just enough so that their thighs brushed. Mikhail wasn't sure if he was more surprised or more amused. But to save her pride, he smiled, easing away slowly. "You have a lovely home. It suits you."

"I'd love to see your studio." Margerite let the invitation melt into her eyes. "Where you create."

"I'm afraid you'd find it cramped, hot and boring."

"Impossible." Smiling, she traced a fingertip over the back of his hand. "I'm sure I'd find nothing about you boring."

Good God, the woman was old enough to be his mother, and she was coming on to him like a misty-eyed virgin primed for her first tumble. Mikhail nearly sighed, then reminded himself it was only a moment out of his life. He took her hand between both of his hands.

"Margerite, you're charming. And I'm—" he kissed her fingers lightly "—unsuitable."

She lifted a finger and brushed it over his cheek. "You underestimate yourself, Mikhail."

No, but he realized how he'd underestimated her.

On the terrace below, Sydney was trying to find a graceful way to discourage Channing. He was attentive, dignified, solicitous, and he was boring her senseless.

It was her lack, she was sure. Any woman with half a soul would be melting under the attraction of a man like Channing. There was moonlight, music, flowers. The breeze in the leafy trees smelled of the sea and murmured of romance. Channing was talking about Paris, and his hand was skimming lightly over her bare back.

She wished she was home, alone, with her eyes crossing over a fat file of quarterly reports.

Taking a deep breath, she turned. She would have to tell him firmly, simply and straight out that he needed to look elsewhere for companionship. It was Sydney's bad luck that she happened to glance up to see Mikhail on the rooftop with her mother just when he took Margerite's hand to his lips.

Why the...she couldn't think of anything vile enough to call him. Slime was too simple. Gigolo too slick. He was nuzzling up to her mother. *Her mother.* When only hours before he'd been...

Nothing, Sydney reminded herself and dismissed the tense scene in the Soho hallway from her mind. He'd been posturing and preening, that was all.

And she could have killed him for it.

As she watched, Mikhail backed away from Margerite, laughing. Then he looked down. The instant their eyes met, Sydney declared war.

She whirled on Channing, her face so fierce he nearly babbled. "Kiss me," she demanded.

"Why, Sydney."

"I said kiss me." She grabbed him by the lapels and hauled him against her.

"Of course, darling." Pleased with her change of heart, he cupped her shoulders in his hands and leaned down to her.

His lips were soft, warm, eager. They slanted over hers with practiced precision while his hands slid down her back. He tasted of after-dinner mints. Her body fit well against his.

And she felt nothing, nothing but an empty inner rage. Then a chill that was both fear and despair.

"You're not trying, darling," he whispered. "You know I won't hurt you."

No, he wouldn't. There was nothing at all to fear from Channing. Miserable, she let him deepen the kiss, ordered herself to feel and respond. She felt his withdrawal even before his lips left hers. The twinges of annoyance and puzzlement.

"Sydney, dear, I'm not sure what the problem is." He smoothed down his crinkled lapels. Marginally frustrated, he lifted his eyes. "That was like kissing my sister."

"I'm tired, Channing," she said to the air between them. "I should go in and get ready to go."

Twenty minutes later, the driver turned the car toward Manhattan. In the back seat Sydney sat ramrod straight well over in her corner, while Mikhail sprawled in his. They didn't bother to speak, not even the polite nonentities of two people who had attended the same function.

He was boiling with rage.

She was frigid with disdain.

She'd done it to annoy him, Mikhail decided. She'd let that silk-suited jerk all but swallow her whole just to make him suffer.

Why was he suffering? he asked himself. She was nothing to him.

No, she was something, he corrected, and brooded into the dark. His only problem was figuring out exactly what that something was.

Obviously, Sydney reflected, the man had no ethics, no morals, no shame. Here he was, just sitting there, all innocence and quiet reflection, after his disgraceful behavior. She frowned at the pale image of her own face in the window glass and tried to listen to the

Chopin prelude on the stereo. Flirting so blatantly with a woman twenty years older. Sneering, yes positively sneering down from the rooftop.

And she'd hired him. Sydney let out a quiet, hissing breath from between her teeth. Oh, that was something she regretted. She'd let her concern, her determination to do the right thing, blind her into hiring some oversexed, amoral Russian carpenter.

Well, if he thought he was going to start playing patty-cake with her mother, he was very much mistaken.

She drew a breath, turned and aimed one steady glare. Mikhail would have sworn the temperature in the car dropped fifty degrees in a snap.

"You stay away from my mother."

He slanted her a look from under his lashes and gracefully crossed his legs. "Excuse me?"

"You heard me, Boris. If you think I'm going to stand by and watch you put the moves on my mother, think again. She's lonely and vulnerable. Her last divorce upset her and she isn't over it."

He said something short and sharp in his native tongue and closed his eyes.

Temper had Sydney sliding across the seat until she could poke his arm. "What the hell does that mean?"

"You want translation? The simplest is bullshit. Now shut up. I'm going to sleep."

"You're not going anywhere until we settle this. You keep your big, grimy hands off my mother, or I'll turn that building you're so fond of into a parking lot."

His eyes slitted open. She found the glitter of angry eyes immensely satisfying. "A big threat from a small woman," he said in a deceptively lazy voice. She was entirely too close for his comfort, and her scent was swimming in his senses, tangling his temper with something more basic. "You should concentrate on the suit, and let your mother handle her own."

"Suit? What suit?"

"The banker who spent the evening sniffing your ankles."

Her face flooded with color. "He certainly was not. He's entirely too well mannered to sniff at my ankles or anything else. And Channing is my business."

"So. You have your business, and I have mine. Now, let's see what we have together." One moment he was stretched out, and the next he had her twisted over his lap. Stunned, Sydney pressed her hands against his chest and tried to struggle out of his hold. He tightened it. "As you see, I have no manners."

"Oh, I know it." She tossed her head back, chin jutting. "What do you think you're doing?"

He wished to hell he knew. She was rigid as an ice floe, but there was something incredible, and Lord, inevitable, about the way she fit into his arms. Though he was cursing himself, he held her close, close enough that he felt the uneven rise and fall of her breasts against his chest, tasted the sweet, wine-tipped flavor of her breath on his lips.

There was a lesson here, he thought grimly, and she was going to learn it.

"I've decided to teach you how to kiss. From what I saw from the roof, you did a poor job of it with the polo player."

Shock and fury had her going still. She would not squirm or scream or give him the satisfaction of frightening her. His eyes were close and challenging.

She thought she understood exactly how Lucifer would have looked as he walked through the gates of his own dark paradise.

"You conceited jerk." Because she wanted to slug him, badly, she fisted her hands closed and looked haughtily down her small, straight nose. "There's nothing you can teach me."

"No?" He wondered if he'd be better off just strangling her and having done with it. "Let's see then. Your Channing put his hands here. Yes?" He slid them over her shoulders. The quick, involuntary shudder chilled her skin. "You afraid of me, *milaya?*"

"Don't be ridiculous." But she was, suddenly and deeply. She swallowed the fear as his thumbs caressed her bare skin.

"Tremble is good. It makes a man feel strong. I don't think you trembled for this Channing."

She said nothing and wondered if he knew his accent had thickened. It sounded exotic, erotic. He wondered he could speak at all with her watching him and waiting.

"His way isn't mine," he muttered. "I'll show you."

His fingers clamped around the back of her neck, pulled her face toward his. He heard her breath catch then shudder out when he paused only a fraction before their lips touched. Her eyes filled his vision, that wide, wary blue. Ignoring the twist in his gut, he smiled, turned his head just an inch and skimmed his lips over her jawline.

She bit back only part of the moan. Instinctively she tipped her head back, giving him access to the long, sensitive column of her throat.

What was he doing to her? Her mind raced frantically to catch up with her soaring body. Why didn't he just get it over with so she could escape with her pride intact?

She'd kill him for this. Crush him. Destroy him.

And oh, it felt wonderful, delicious. Wicked.

He could only think she tasted of morning—cool, spring mornings when the dew slicked over green, green grass and new flowers. She shivered against him, her body still held stiffly away even as her head fell back in surrender.

Who was she? He nibbled lazily over to her ear and burned for her to show him.

A thousand, a million pinpricks of pleasure danced along her skin. Shaken by them, she started to pull away. But his hands slid down her back and melted her spine. All the while his lips teased and tormented, never, never coming against hers to relieve the aching pressure.

She wanted.

The slow, flickering heat kindling in the pit of her stomach.

She yearned.

Spreading, spreading through her blood and bone.

She needed.

Wave after wave of liquid fire lapping, cruising, flowing over her skin.

She took.

In a fire flash her system exploded. Mouth to mouth she strained against him, pressing ice to heat and letting it steam until the air was so thick with it, it clogged in her throat. Her fingers speared through his hair and fisted as she fed greedily on the stunning flavor of her own passion.

This. At last this. He was rough and restless and smelled of man instead of expensive colognes. The words he muttered were incomprehensible against her mouth. But they didn't sound like endearments, reassurances, promises. They sounded like threats.

His mouth wasn't soft and warm and eager, but hot and hard and ruthless. She wanted that, how she wanted the heedless and hasty meeting of lips and tongues.

His hands weren't hesitant or practiced, but strong and impatient. It ran giddily through her brain that he would take what he wanted, when and where it suited him. The pleasure and power of it burst through her like sunlight. She choked out his name when he tugged her bodice down and filled his calloused hands with her breasts.

He was drowning in her. The ice had melted and he was over his head, too dazed to know if he should dive deeper or scrabble for the surface. The scent, the taste, oh Lord, the texture. Alabaster and silk and rose petals. Every fine thing a man could want to touch, to steal, to claim as his own. His hands raced over her as he fought for more.

On an oath he shifted, and she was under him on the long plush seat of the car, her hair spread out like melted copper, her body moving, moving under his, her white breasts spilling out above the stark black dress and tormenting him into tasting.

She arched, and her fingers dug into his back as he suckled. A deep and delicious ache tugged at the center of her body. And she wanted him there, there where the heat was most intense. There where she felt so soft, so needy.

"Please." She could hear the whimper in her voice but felt no embarrassment. Only desperation. "Mikhail, please."

The throaty purr of her voice burst in his blood. He came back to her mouth, assaulting it, devouring it. Crazed, he hooked one hand in the top of her dress, on the verge of ripping it from her. And he looked, looked at her face, the huge eyes, the trembling lips. Light and shadow washed over it, leaving her pale as a ghost. She was shaking like a leaf beneath his hands.

And he heard the drum of traffic from outside.

He surfaced abruptly, shaking his head to clear it and gulping in air like a diver down too long. They were driving through the city, their privacy as thin as the panel of smoked glass that separated them from her chauffeur. And he was mauling her, yes, mauling her as if he were a reckless teenager with none of the sense God had given him.

The apology stuck in his throat. An "I beg your pardon" would hardly do the trick. Eyes grim, loins aching, he tugged her dress back into place. She only stared at him and made him feel like a drooling heathen over a virgin sacrifice. And Lord help him, he wanted to plunder.

Swearing, he pushed away and yanked her upright. He leaned back in the shadows and stared out of the dark window. They were only blocks from his apartment. Blocks, and he'd very nearly... it wouldn't do to think about what he'd nearly.

"We're almost there." Strain had his voice coming out clipped and hard. Sydney winced away as though it had been a slap.

What had she done wrong this time? She'd felt, and she'd wanted. Felt and wanted more than she ever had before. Yet she had still failed. For that one timeless moment she'd been willing to toss aside pride and fear. There had been passion in her, real and ready. And, she'd thought, he'd felt passion for her.

But not enough. She closed her eyes. It never seemed to be enough. Now she was cold, freezing, and wrapped her arms tight to try to hold in some remnant of heat.

Damn it, why didn't she say something? Mikhail dragged an unsteady hand through his hair. He deserved to be slapped. Shot was more like it. And she just sat there.

As he brooded out the window, he reminded himself that it hadn't been all his doing. She'd been as rash, pressing that wonderful body against his, letting that wide, mobile mouth make him crazy. Squirting that damnable perfume all over that soft skin until he'd been drunk with it.

He started to feel better.

Yes, there had been two people grappling in the back seat. She was every bit as guilty as he.

"Look, Sydney." He turned and she jerked back like an overwound spring.

"Don't touch me." He heard only the venom and none of the tears.

"Fine." Guilt hammered away at him as the car cruised to the curb. "I'll keep my big, grimy hands off you, Hayward. Call someone else when you want a little romp in the back seat."

Her fisted hands held on to pride and composure. "I meant what I said about my mother."

He shoved the door open. Light spilled in, splashing over his face, turning it frosty white. "So did I. Thanks for the ride."

When the door slammed, she closed her eyes tight. She would not cry. A single tear slipped past her guard and was dashed away. She would not cry. And she would not forget.

Chapter Four

She'd put in a long day. Actually she'd put in a long week that was edging toward sixty hours between office time, luncheon meetings and evenings at home with files. This particular day had a few hours yet to run, but Sydney recognized the new feeling of relief and satisfaction that came with Friday afternoons when the work force began to anticipate Saturday mornings.

Throughout her adult life one day of the week had been the same as the next; all of them a scattershot of charity functions, shopping and lunch dates. There had been no work schedule, and weekends had simply been a time when the parties had lasted longer.

Things had changed. As she read over a new contract, she was glad they had. She was beginning to understand why her grandfather had always been so lusty and full of life. He'd had a purpose, a place, a goal.

Now they were hers.

True, she still had to ask advice on the more technical wordings of contracts and depended heavily on her board when it came to making deals. But she was starting to appreciate—more, she was starting to relish the grand chess game of buying and selling buildings.

She circled what she considered a badly worded clause then answered her intercom.

"Mr. Bingham to see you, Ms. Hayward."

"Send him in, Janine. Oh, and see if you can reach Frank Marlowe at Marlowe, Radcliffe and Smyth."

"Yes, ma'am."

When Lloyd strode in a moment later, Sydney was still huddled over the contract. She held up one finger to give herself a minute to finish.

"Lloyd. I'm sorry, if I lose my concentration on all these *whereas*es, I have to start over." She scrawled a note to herself, set it and the contract aside, then smiled at him. "What can I do for you?"

"This Soho project. It's gotten entirely out of hand."

Her lips tightened. Thinking of Soho made her think of Mikhail. Mikhail reminded her of the turbulent ride from Long Island and her latest failure as a woman. She didn't care for it.

"In what way?"

"In every way." With fury barely leashed, he began to pace her office. "A quarter of a million. You earmarked a quarter of a million to rehab that building."

Sydney stayed where she was and quietly folded her hands on the desk. "I'm aware of that, Lloyd. Considering the condition of the building, Mr. Stanislaski's bid was very reasonable."

"How would you know?" he shot back. "Did you get competing bids?"

"No." Her fingers flexed, then relaxed again. It was difficult, but she reminded herself that he'd earned his way up the ladder while she'd been hoisted to the top rung. "I went with my instincts."

"Instincts?" Eyes narrowed, he spun back to her. The derision in his voice was as thick as the pile of her carpet. "You've been in the business for a matter of months, and you have instincts."

"That's right. I'm also aware that the estimate for rewiring, the plumbing and the carpentry were well in line with other, similar rehabs."

"Damn it, Sydney, we didn't put much more than that into this building last year."

One slim finger began to tap on the desk. "What we did here in the Hayward Building was little more than decorating. A good many of the repairs in Soho are a matter of safety and bringing the facilities up to code."

"A quarter of a million in repairs." He slapped his palms on the desk and leaned forward. Sydney was reminded of Mikhail making a similar gesture. But of course Lloyd's hands would leave no smudge of dirt. "Do you know what our annual income is from those apartments?"

"As a matter of fact I do." She rattled off a figure, surprising him. It was accurate to the penny. "On one hand, it will certainly take more than a year of full occupancy to recoup the principal on this investment.

On the other, when people pay rent in good faith, they deserve decent housing."

"Decent, certainly," Lloyd said stiffly. "You're mixing morals with business."

"Oh, I hope so. I certainly hope so."

He drew back, infuriated that she would sit so smug and righteous behind a desk that should have been his. "You're naive, Sydney."

"That may be. But as long as I run this company, it will be run by my standards."

"You think you run it because you sign a few contracts and make phone calls. You've put a quarter million into what you yourself termed your pet project, and you don't have a clue what this Stanislaski's up to. How do you know he isn't buying inferior grades and pocketing the excess?"

"That's absurd."

"As I said, you're naive. You put some Russian artist in charge of a major project, then don't even bother to check the work."

"I intend to inspect the project myself. I've been tied up. And I have Mr. Stanislaski's weekly report."

He sneered. Before Sydney's temper could fray, she realized Lloyd was right. She'd hired Mikhail on impulse and instinct, then because of personal feelings, had neglected to follow through with her involvement on the project.

That wasn't naive. It was gutless.

"You're absolutely right, Lloyd, and I'll correct it." She leaned back in her chair. "Was there anything else?"

"You've made a mistake," he said. "A costly one in this case. The board won't tolerate another."

With her hands laid lightly on the arms of her chair, she nodded. "And you're hoping to convince them that you belong at this desk."

"They're businessmen, Sydney. And though sentiment might prefer a Hayward at the head of the table, profit and loss will turn the tide."

Her expression remained placid, her voice steady. "I'm sure you're right again. And if the board continues to back me, I want one of two things from you. Your resignation or your loyalty. I won't accept anything in between. Now, if you'll excuse me?"

When the door slammed behind him, she reached for the phone. But her hand was trembling, and she drew it back. She plucked up a paper clip and mangled it. Then another, then a third. Between that and the two sheets of stationery she shredded, she felt the worst of the rage subside.

Clearheaded, she faced the facts.

Lloyd Bingham was an enemy, and he was an enemy with experience and influence. She had acted in haste with Soho. Not that she'd been wrong; she didn't believe she'd been wrong. But if there were mistakes, Lloyd would capitalize on them and drop them right in her lap.

Was it possible that she was risking everything her grandfather had given her with one project? Could she be forced to step down if she couldn't prove the worth and right of what she had done?

She wasn't sure, and that was the worst of it.

One step at a time. That was the only way to go on. And the first step was to get down to Soho and do her job.

* * *

The sky was the color of drywall. Over the past few days, the heat had ebbed, but it had flowed back into the city that morning like a river, flooding Manhattan with humidity. The pedestrian traffic surged through it, streaming across the intersections in hot little packs.

Girls in shorts and men in wilted business suits crowded around the sidewalk vendors in hopes that an ice-cream bar or a soft drink would help them beat the heat.

When Sydney stepped out of her car, the sticky oppression of the air punched like a fist. She thought of her driver sitting in the enclosed car and dismissed him for the day. Shielding her eyes, she turned to study her building.

Scaffolding crept up the walls like metal ivy. Windows glittered, their manufacturer stickers slashed across the glass. She thought she saw a pair of arthritic hands scraping away at a label at a third-floor window.

There were signs in the doorway, warning of construction in progress. She could hear the sounds of it, booming hammers, buzzing saws, the clang of metal and the tinny sound of rock and roll through portable speakers.

At the curb she saw the plumber's van, a dented pickup and a scattering of interested onlookers. Since they were all peering up, she followed their direction. And saw Mikhail.

For an instant, her heart stopped dead. He stood outside the top floor, five stories up, moving nimbly on what seemed to Sydney to be a very narrow board.

"Man, get a load of those buns," a woman beside her sighed. "They are class A."

Sydney swallowed. She supposed they were. And his naked back wasn't anything to sneeze at, either. The trouble was, it was hard to enjoy it when she had a hideous flash of him plummeting off the scaffolding and breaking that beautiful back on the concrete below.

Panicked, she rushed inside. The elevator doors were open, and a couple of mechanics were either loading or unloading their tools inside it. She didn't stop to ask but bolted up the steps.

Sweaty men were replastering the stairwell between two and three. They took the time to whistle and wink, but she kept climbing. Someone had the television up too loud, probably to drown out the sound of construction. A baby was crying fitfully. She smelled chicken frying.

Without pausing for breath, she dashed from four to five. There was music playing here. Tough and gritty rock, poorly accompanied by a laborer in an off-key tenor.

Mikhail's door was open, and Sydney streaked through. She nearly tumbled over a graying man with arms like tree trunks. He rose gracefully from his crouched position where he'd been sorting tools and steadied her.

"I'm sorry. I didn't see you."

"Is all right. I like women to fall at my feet."

She registered the Slavic accent even as she glanced desperately around the room for Mikhail. Maybe everybody in the building was Russian, she thought frantically. Maybe he'd imported plumbers from the mother country.

"Can I help you?"

"No. Yes." She pressed a hand to her heart when she realized she was completely out of breath. "Mikhail."

"He is just outside." Intrigued, he watched her as he jerked a thumb toward the window.

She could see him there—at least she could see the flat, tanned torso. "Outside. But, but—"

"We are finishing for the day. You will sit?"

"Get him in," Sydney whispered. "Please, get him in."

Before he could respond, the window was sliding up, and Mikhail was tossing one long, muscled leg inside. He said something in his native tongue, laughter in his voice as the rest of his body followed. When he saw Sydney, the laughter vanished.

"Hayward." He tapped his caulking gun against his palm.

"What were you doing out there?" The question came out in an accusing rush.

"Replacing windows." He set the caulking gun aside. "Is there a problem?"

"No, I…" She couldn't remember ever feeling more of a fool. "I came by to check the progress."

"So. I'll take you around in a minute." He walked into the kitchen, stuck his head into the sink and turned the faucet on full cold.

"He's a hothead," the man behind her said, chuckling at his own humor. When Sydney only managed a weak smile, he called out to Mikhail, speaking rapidly in that exotic foreign tongue.

"Tak" was all he said. Mikhail came up dripping, hair streaming over the bandanna he'd tied around it. He shook it back, splattering water, then shrugged and hooked his thumbs in his belt loops. He was wet, sweaty and half-naked. Sydney had to fold her tongue inside her mouth to keep it from hanging out.

"My son is rude." Yuri Stanislaski shook his head. "I raised him better."

"Your—oh." Sydney looked back at the man with the broad face and beautiful hands. Mikhail's hands. "How do you do, Mr. Stanislaski."

"I do well. I am Yuri. I ask my son if you are the Hayward who owns this business. He only says yes and scowls."

"Yes, well, I am."

"It's a good building. Only a little sick. And we are the doctors." He grinned at his son, then boomed out something else in Ukrainian.

This time an answering smile tugged at Mikhail's mouth. "No, you haven't lost a patient yet, Papa. Go home and have your dinner."

Yuri hauled up his tool chest. "You come and bring the pretty lady. Your mama makes enough."

"Oh, well, thank you, but—"

"I'm busy tonight, Papa." Mikhail cut off Sydney's polite refusal.

Yuri raised a bushy brow. "You're stupid tonight," he said in Ukrainian. "Is this the one who makes you sulk all week?"

Annoyed, Mikhail picked up a kitchen towel and wiped his face. "Women don't make me sulk."

Yuri only smiled. "This one would." Then he turned to Sydney. "Now I am rude, too, talking so you

don't understand. He is bad influence." He lifted her
hand and kissed it with considerable charm. "I am
glad to meet you."

"I'm glad to meet you, too."

"Put on a shirt," Yuri ordered his son, then left,
whistling.

"He's very nice," Sydney said.

"Yes." Mikhail picked up the T-shirt he'd peeled off
hours before, but only held it. "So, you want to see the
work?"

"Yes, I thought—"

"The windows are done," he interrupted. "The
wiring is almost done. That and the plumbing will take
another week. Come."

He moved out, skirting her by a good two feet, then
walked into the apartment next door without knocking.

"Keely's," he told her. "She is out."

The room was a clash of sharp colors and scents.
The furniture was old and sagging but covered with
vivid pillows and various articles of female attire.

The adjoining kitchen was a mess—not with dishes
or pots and pans—but with walls torn down to studs
and thick wires snaked through.

"It must be inconvenient for her, for everyone,
during the construction."

"Better than plugging in a cake mixer and shorting
out the building. The old wire was tube and knob,
forty years old or more, and frayed. This is Romex.
More efficient, safer."

She bent over his arm, studying the wiring. "Well.
Hmm."

He nearly smiled. Perhaps he would have if she hadn't smelled so good. Instead, he moved a deliberate foot away. "After the inspection, we will put up new walls. Come."

It was a trial for both of them, but he took her through every stage of the work, moving from floor to floor, showing her elbows of plastic pipe and yards of copper tubing.

"Most of the flooring can be saved with sanding and refinishing. But some must be replaced." He kicked at a square of plywood he'd nailed to a hole in the second-floor landing.

Sydney merely nodded, asking questions only when they seemed intelligent. Most of the workers were gone, off to cash their week's paychecks. The noise level had lowered so that she could hear muted voices behind closed doors, snatches of music or televised car chases. She lifted a brow at the sound of a tenor sax swinging into "Rhapsody in Blue."

"That's Will Metcalf," Mikhail told her. "He's good. Plays in a band."

"Yes, he's good." The rail felt smooth and sturdy under her hand as they went down. Mikhail had done that, she thought. He'd fixed, repaired, replaced, as needed because he cared about the people who lived in the building. He knew who was playing the sax or eating the fried chicken, whose baby was laughing.

"Are you happy with the progress?" she asked quietly.

The tone of her voice made him look at her, something he'd been trying to avoid. A few tendrils of hair had escaped their pins to curl at her temples. He could see a pale dusting of freckles across her nose. "Happy enough. It's you who should answer. It's your building."

"No, it's not." Her eyes were very serious, very sad. "It's yours. I only write the checks."

"Sydney—"

"I've seen enough to know you've made a good start." She was hurrying down the steps as she spoke. "Be sure to contact my office when it's time for the next draw."

"Damn it. Slow down." He caught up with her at the bottom of the steps and grabbed her arm. "What's wrong with you? First you stand in my room pale and out of breath. Now you run away, and your eyes are miserable."

It had hit her, hard, that she had no community of people who cared. Her circle of friends was so narrow, so self-involved. Her best friend had been Peter, and that had been horribly spoiled. Her life was on the sidelines, and she envied the involvement, the closeness she felt in this place. The building wasn't hers, she thought again. She only owned it.

"I'm not running away, and nothing's wrong with me." She had to get out, get away, but she had to do it with dignity. "I take this job very seriously. It's my first major project since taking over Hayward. I want it done right. And I took a chance by..." She trailed off, glancing toward the door just to her right. She could have sworn she'd heard someone call for help. Television, she thought, but before she could continue, she heard the thin, pitiful call again. "Mikhail, do you hear that?"

"Hear what?" How could he hear anything when he was trying not to kiss her again?

"In here." She turned toward the door, straining her ears. "Yes, in here, I heard—"

That time he'd heard it, too. Lifting a fist, he pounded on the door. "Mrs. Wolburg. Mrs. Wolburg, it's Mik."

The shaky voice barely penetrated the wood. "Hurt. Help me."

"Oh, God, she's—"

Before Sydney could finish, Mikhail rammed his shoulder against the door. With the second thud, it crashed open to lean drunkenly on its hinges.

"In the kitchen," Mrs. Wolburg called weakly. "Mik, thank God."

He bolted through the apartment with its starched doilies and paper flowers to find her on the kitchen floor. She was a tiny woman, mostly bone and thin flesh. Her usually neat cap of white hair was matted with sweat.

"Can't see," she said. "Dropped my glasses."

"Don't worry." He knelt beside her, automatically checking her pulse as he studied her pain-filled eyes. "Call an ambulance," he ordered Sydney, but she was already on the phone. "I'm not going to help you up, because I don't know how you're hurt."

"Hip." She gritted her teeth at the awful, radiating pain. "I think I busted my hip. Fell, caught my foot. Couldn't move. All the noise, nobody could hear me calling. Been here two, three hours. Got so weak."

"It's all right now." He tried to chafe some heat into her hands. "Sydney, get a blanket and pillow."

She had them in her arms and was already crouching beside Mrs. Wolburg before he'd finished the order. "Here now. I'm just going to lift your head a little." Gently she set the woman's limp head on the pillow. Despite the raging heat, Mrs. Wolburg was shivering with cold. As she continued to speak in quiet, soothing tones, Sydney tucked the blanket around her. "Just a few more minutes," Sydney murmured, and stroked the clammy forehead.

A crowd was forming at the door. Though he didn't like leaving Sydney with the injured woman, he rose. "I want to keep the neighbors away. Send someone to keep an eye for the ambulance."

"Fine." While fear pumped hard in her heart, she continued to smile down at Mrs. Wolburg. "You have a lovely apartment. Do you crochet the doilies yourself?"

"Been doing needlework for sixty years, since I was pregnant with my first daughter."

"They're beautiful. Do you have other children?"

"Six, three of each. And twenty grandchildren. Five great..." She shut her eyes on a flood of pain, then opened them again and managed a smile. "Been after me for living alone, but I like my own place and my own way."

"Of course."

"And my daughter, Lizzy? Moved clear out to Phoenix, Arizona. Now what would I want to live out there for?"

Sydney smiled and stroked. "I couldn't say."

"They'll be on me now," she muttered, and let her eyes close again. "Wouldn't have happened if I hadn't dropped my glasses. Terrible nearsighted. Getting old's hell, girl, and don't let anyone tell you different. Couldn't see where I was going and snagged my foot in that torn linoleum. Mik told me to keep it taped down, but I wanted to give it a good scrub." She managed a wavery smile. "Least I've been lying here on a clean floor."

"Paramedics are coming up," Mikhail said from behind her. Sydney only nodded, filled with a terrible guilt and anger she was afraid to voice.

"You call my grandson, Mik? He lives up on Eighty-first. He'll take care of the rest of the family."

"Don't worry about it, Mrs. Wolburg."

Fifteen efficient minutes later, Sydney stood on the sidewalk watching as the stretcher was lifted into the back of the ambulance.

"Did you reach her grandson?" she asked Mikhail.

"I left a message on his machine."

Nodding, she walked to the curb and tried to hail a cab.

"Where's your car?"

"I sent him home. I didn't know how long I'd be and it was too hot to leave him sitting there. Maybe I should go back in and call a cab."

"In a hurry?"

She winced as the siren shrieked. "I want to get to the hospital."

Nonplussed, he jammed his hands into his pockets. "There's no need for you to go."

She turned, and her eyes, in the brief moment they held his, were ripe with emotion. Saying nothing, she faced away until a cab finally swung to the curb. Nor did she speak when Mikhail climbed in behind her.

* * *

She hated the smell of hospitals. Layers of illness, antiseptics, fear and heavy cleaners. The memory of the last days her grandfather had lain dying were still too fresh in her mind. The Emergency Room of the downtown hospital added one more layer. Fresh blood.

Sydney steeled herself against it and walked through the crowds of the sick and injured to the admitting window.

"You had a Mrs. Wolburg just come in."

"That's right." The clerk stabbed keys on her computer. "You family?"

"No, I—"

"We're going to need some family to fill out these forms. Patient said she wasn't insured."

Mikhail was already leaning over, eyes dangerous, when Sydney snapped out her answer. "Hayward Industries will be responsible for Mrs. Wolburg's medical expenses." She reached into her bag for identification and slapped it onto the counter. "I'm Sydney Hayward. Where is Mrs. Wolburg?"

"In X ray." The frost in Sydney's eyes had the clerk shifting in her chair. "Dr. Cohen's attending."

So they waited, drinking bad coffee among the moans and tears of inner city ER. Sometimes Sydney would lay her head back against the wall and shut her eyes. She appeared to be dozing, but all the while she was thinking what it would be like to be old, and alone and helpless.

He wanted to think she was only there to cover her butt. Oh yes, he wanted to think that of her. It was so much more comfortable to think of her as the head of some bloodless company than as a woman.

But he remembered how quickly she had acted in the Wolburg apartment, how gentle she had been with the old woman. And most of all, he remembered the look in her eyes out on the street. All that misery and compassion and guilt welling up in those big eyes.

"She tripped on the linoleum," Sydney murmured.

It was the first time she'd spoken in nearly an hour, and Mikhail turned his head to study her. Her eyes were still closed, her face pale and in repose.

"She was only walking in her own kitchen and fell because the floor was old and unsafe."

"You're making it safe."

Sydney continued as if she hadn't heard. "Then she could only lie there, hurt and alone. Her voice was so weak. I nearly walked right by."

"You didn't walk by." His hand hesitated over hers. Then, with an oath, he pressed his palm to the back of her hand. "You're only one Hayward, Sydney. Your grandfather—"

"He was ill." Her hand clenched under Mikhail's, and her eyes squeezed more tightly closed. "He was sick nearly two years, and I was in Europe. I didn't know. He didn't want to disrupt my life. My father was dead, and there was only me, and he didn't want to worry me. When he finally called me, it was almost over. He was a good man. He wouldn't have let things get so bad, but he couldn't . . . he just couldn't."

She let out a short, shuddering breath. Mikhail turned her hand over and linked his fingers with hers.

"When I got to New York, he was in the hospital. He looked so small, so tired. He told me I was the only Hayward left. Then he died," she said wearily. "And I was."

"You're doing what needs to be done. No one can ask for more than that."

She opened her eyes again, met his. "I don't know."

They waited again, in silence.

It was nearly two hours before Mrs. Wolburg's frantic grandson rushed in. The entire story had to be told again before he hurried off to call the rest of his family.

Four hours after they'd walked into Emergency, the doctor came out to fill them in.

A fractured hip, a mild concussion. She would be moved to a room right after she'd finished in Recovery. Her age made the break serious, but her health helped balance that. Sydney left both her office and home numbers with the doctor and the grandson, requesting to be kept informed of Mrs. Wolburg's condition.

Unbearably weary in body and mind, Sydney walked out of the hospital.

"You need food," Mikhail said.

"What? No, really, I'm just tired."

Ignoring that, he grabbed her arm and pulled her down the street. "Why do you always say the opposite of what I say?"

"I don't."

"See, you did it again. You need meat."

If she kept trying to drag her heels, he was going to pull her arm right out of the socket. Annoyed, she scrambled to keep pace. "What makes you think you know what I need?"

"Because I do." He pulled up short at a light and she bumped into him. Before he could stop it, his hand had lifted to touch her face. "God, you're so beautiful."

While she blinked in surprise, he swore, scowled then dragged her into the street seconds before the light turned.

"Maybe I'm not happy with you," he went on, muttering to himself. "Maybe I think you're a nuisance, and a snob, and—"

"I am not a snob."

He said something vaguely familiar in his native language. Sydney's chin set when she recalled the translation. "It is not bull. You're the snob if you think I am just because I come from a different background."

He stopped, eyeing her with a mixture of distrust and interest. "Fine then, you won't mind eating in here." He yanked her into a noisy bar and grill. She found herself plopped down in a narrow booth with him, hip to hip.

There were scents of meat cooking, onions frying, spilled beer, all overlaid with grease. Her mouth watered. "I said I wasn't hungry."

"And I say you're a snob, and a liar."

The color that stung her cheeks pleased him, but it didn't last long enough. She leaned forward. "And would you like to know what I think of you?"

Again he lifted a hand to touch her cheek. It was irresistible. "Yes, I would."

She was saved from finding a description in her suddenly murky brain by the waitress.

"Two steaks, medium rare, and two of what you've got on tap."

"I don't like men to order for me," Sydney said tightly.

"Then you can order for me next time and we'll be even." Making himself comfortable, he tossed his arm over the back of the booth and stretched out his legs. "Why don't you take off your jacket, Hayward? You're hot."

"Stop telling me what I am. And stop that, too."

"What?"

"Playing with my hair."

He grinned. "I was playing with your neck. I like your neck." To prove it, he skimmed a finger down it again.

She clamped her teeth on the delicious shudder that followed it down her spine. "I wish you'd move over."

"Okay." He shifted closer. "Better?"

Calm, she told herself. She would be calm. After a cleansing breath, she turned her head. "If you don't..." And his lips brushed over hers, stopping the words and the thought behind them.

"I want you to kiss me back."

She started to shake her head, but couldn't manage it.

"I want to watch you when you do," he murmured. "I want to know what's there."

"There's nothing there."

But his mouth closed over hers and proved her a liar. She fell into the kiss, one hand lost in his hair, the other clamped on his shoulder.

She felt everything. Everything. And it all moved too fast. Her mind seemed to dim until she could barely hear the clatter and bustle of the bar. But she felt his mouth angle over hers, his teeth nip, his tongue seduce.

Whatever she was doing to him, he was doing to her. He knew it. He saw it in the way her eyes glazed before they closed, felt it in the hot, ready passion of her lips. It was supposed to soothe his ego, prove a point. But it did neither.

It only left him aching.

"Sorry to break this up." The waitress slapped two frosted mugs on the table. "Steak's on its way."

Sydney jerked her head back. His arms were still around her, though his grip had loosened. And she, she was plastered against him. Her body molded to his as they sat in a booth in a public place. Shame and fury battled for supremacy as she yanked herself away.

"That was a despicable thing to do."

He shrugged and picked up his beer. "I didn't do it alone." Over the foam, his eyes sharpened. "Not this time, or last time."

"Last time, you . . ."

"What?"

Sydney lifted her mug and sipped gingerly. "I don't want to discuss it."

He wanted to argue, even started to, but there was a sheen of hurt in her eyes that baffled him. He didn't mind making her angry. Hell, he enjoyed it. But he didn't know what he'd done to make her hurt. He waited until the waitress had set the steaks in front of them.

''You've had a rough day,'' he said so kindly Sydney gasped. ''I don't mean to make it worse.''

''It's...'' She struggled with a response. ''It's been a rough day all around. Let's just put it behind us.''

''Done.'' Smiling, he handed her a knife and fork. ''Eat your dinner. We'll have a truce.''

''Good.'' She discovered she had an appetite after all.

Chapter Five

Sydney didn't know how Mildred Wolburg's accident had leaked to the press, but by Tuesday afternoon her office was flooded with calls from reporters. A few of the more enterprising staked out the lobby of the Hayward Building and cornered her when she left for the day.

By Wednesday rumors were flying around the offices that Hayward was facing a multimillion-dollar suit, and Sydney had several unhappy board members on her hands. The consensus was that by assuming responsibility for Mrs. Wolburg's medical expenses, Sydney had admitted Hayward's neglect and had set the company up for a large public settlement.

It was bad press, and bad business.

Knowing no route but the direct one, Sydney prepared a statement for the press and agreed to an emergency board meeting. By Friday, she thought as she walked into the hospital, she would know if she would remain in charge of Hayward or whether her position would be whittled down to figurehead.

Carrying a stack of paperbacks in one hand and a potted plant in the other, Sydney paused outside of Mrs. Wolburg's room. Because it was Sydney's third visit since the accident, she knew the widow wasn't likely to be alone. Invariably, friends and family streamed in and out during visiting hours. This time she saw Mikhail, Keely and two of Mrs. Wolburg's children.

Mikhail spotted her as Sydney was debating whether to slip out again and leave the books and plant she'd brought at the nurse's station.

''You have more company, Mrs. Wolburg.''

''Sydney.'' The widow's eyes brightened behind her thick lenses. ''More books.''

''Your grandson told me you liked to read.'' Feeling awkward, she set the books on the table beside the bed and took Mrs. Wolburg's outstretched hand.

''My Harry used to say I'd rather read than eat.'' The thin, bony fingers squeezed Sydney's. ''That's a beautiful plant.''

''I noticed you have several in your apartment.'' She smiled, feeling slightly more relaxed as the conversation in the room picked up again to flow around them. ''And the last time I was here the room looked like a florist's shop.'' She glanced around at the banks of cut flowers in vases, pots, baskets, even in a ceramic shoe. ''So I settled on an African violet.''

"I do have a weakness for flowers and growing things. Set it right there on the dresser, will you, dear? Between the roses and the carnations."

"She's getting spoiled." As Sydney moved to comply, the visiting daughter winked at her brother. "Flowers, presents, pampering. We'll be lucky to ever get home-baked cookies again."

"Oh, I might have a batch or two left in me." Mrs. Wolburg preened in her new crocheted bed jacket. "Mik tells me I'm getting a brand-new oven. Eye level, so I won't have to bend and stoop."

"So I think I should get the first batch," Mikhail said as he sniffed the roses. "The chocolate chip."

"Please." Keely pressed a hand to her stomach. "I'm dieting. I'm getting murdered next week, and I have to look my best." She noted Sydney's stunned expression and grinned. *"Death Stalk,"* she explained. "My first TV movie. I'm the third victim of the maniacal psychopath. I get strangled in this really terrific negligee."

"You shouldn't have left your windows unlocked," Mrs. Wolburg told her, and Keely grinned again.

"Well, that's show biz."

Sydney waited until a break in the conversation, then made her excuses. Mikhail gave her a ten-second lead before he slipped a yellow rose out of a vase. "See you later, beautiful." He kissed Mrs. Wolburg on the cheek and left her chuckling.

In a few long strides, he caught up with Sydney at the elevators. "Hey. You look like you could use this." He offered the flower.

"It couldn't hurt." After sniffing the bloom, she worked up a smile. "Thanks."

"You want to tell me why you're upset?"

"I'm not upset." She jabbed the down button again.

"Never argue with an artist about your feelings." Insistently he tipped back her chin with one finger. "I see fatigue and distress, worry and annoyance."

The ding of the elevator relieved her, though she knew he would step inside the crowded car with her. She frowned a little when she found herself pressed between Mikhail and a large woman carrying a suitcase-sized purse. Someone on the elevator had used an excess of expensive perfume. Fleetingly Sydney wondered if that shouldn't be as illegal as smoking in a closed car.

"Any Gypsies in your family?" she asked Mikhail on impulse.

"Naturally."

"I'd rather you use a crystal ball to figure out the future than analyze my feelings at the moment."

"We'll see what we can do."

The car stopped on each floor. People shuffled off or squeezed in. By the time they reached the lobby, Sydney was hard up against Mikhail's side, with his arm casually around her waist. He didn't bother to remove it after they'd stepped off. She didn't bother to mention it.

"The work's going well," he told her.

"Good." She didn't care to think how much longer she'd be directly involved with the project.

"The electrical inspection is done. Plumbing will perhaps take another week." He studied her abstracted expression. "And we have decided to make the new roof out of blue cheese."

"Hmm." She stepped outside, stopped and looked back at him. With a quick laugh, she shook her head. "That might look very distinctive—but risky with this heat."

"You were listening."

"Almost." Absently she pressed fingers to her throbbing temple as her driver pulled up to the curb. "I'm sorry. I've got a lot on my mind."

"Tell me."

It surprised her that she wanted to. She hadn't been able to talk to her mother. Margerite would only be baffled. Channing—that was a joke. Sydney doubted that any of her friends would understand how she had become so attached to Hayward in such a short time.

"There really isn't any point," she decided, and started toward her waiting car and driver.

Did she think he would let her walk away, with that worry line between her brows and the tension knotted tight in her shoulders?

"How about a lift home?"

She glanced back. The ride home from her mother's party was still a raw memory. But he was smiling at her in an easy, friendly fashion. Nonthreatening? No, he would never be that with those dark looks and untamed aura. But they had agreed on a truce, and it was only a few blocks.

"Sure. We'll drop Mr. Stanislaski off in Soho, Donald."

"Yes, ma'am."

She took the precaution of sliding, casually, she hoped, all the way over to the far window. "Mrs.

Wolburg looks amazingly well, considering," she began.

"She's strong." It was Mozart this time, he noted, low and sweet through the car speakers.

"The doctor says she'll be able to go home with her son soon."

"And you've arranged for the therapist to visit." Sydney stopped passing the rose from hand to hand and looked at him. "She told me," he explained. "Also that when she is ready to go home again, there will be a nurse to stay with her, until she is well enough to be on her own."

"I'm not playing Samaritan," Sydney mumbled. "I'm just trying to do what's right."

"I realize that. I realize, too, that you're concerned for her. But there's something more on your mind. Is it the papers and the television news?"

Her eyes went from troubled to frigid. "I didn't assume responsibility for Mrs. Wolburg's medical expenses for publicity, good or bad. And I don't—"

"I know you didn't." He cupped a hand over one of her clenched ones. "Remember, I was there. I saw you with her."

Sydney drew a deep breath. She had to. She'd very nearly had a tirade, and a lost temper was hardly the answer. "The point is," she said more calmly, "an elderly woman was seriously injured. Her pain shouldn't become company politics or journalistic fodder. What I did, I did because I knew it was right. I just want to make sure the right thing continues to be done."

"You are president of Hayward."

"For the moment." She turned to look out the window as they pulled up in front of the apartment building. "I see we're making progress on the roof."

"Among other things." Because he was far from finished, he leaned over her and opened the door on her side. For a moment, they were so close, his body pressed lightly to hers. She had an urge, almost desperate, to rub her fingers over his cheek, to feel the rough stubble he'd neglected to shave away. "I'd like you to come up," he told her. "I have something for you."

Sydney caught her fingers creeping up and snatched them back. "It's nearly six. I really should—"

"Come up for an hour," he finished. "Your driver can come back for you, yes?"

"Yes." She shifted away, not sure whether she wanted to get out or simply create some distance between them. "You can messenger your report over."

"I could."

He moved another inch. In defense, Sydney swung her legs out of the car. "All right then, but I don't think it'll take an hour."

"But it will."

She relented because she preferred spending an hour going over a report than sitting in her empty apartment thinking about the scheduled board meeting. After giving her driver instructions, she walked with Mikhail toward the building.

"You've repaired the stoop."

"Tuesday. It wasn't easy getting the men to stop sitting on it long enough." He exchanged greetings with the three who were ranged across it now as Sydney passed through the aroma of beer and tobacco.

"We can take the elevator. The inspection certificate is hardly dry."

She thought of the five long flights up. "I can't tell you how glad I am to hear that." She stepped in with him, waited while he pulled the open iron doors closed.

"It has character now," he said as they began the assent. "And you don't worry that you'll get in to get downstairs and spend the night inside."

"There's good news."

He pulled the doors open again as the car slid to a smooth, quiet stop. In the hallway, the ceiling was gone, leaving bare joists and new wiring exposed.

"The water damage from leaking was bad," Mikhail said conversationally. "Once the roof is finished, we'll replace."

"I've expected some complaints from the tenants, but we haven't received a single one. Isn't it difficult for everyone, living in a construction zone?"

Mikhail jingled his keys. "Inconvenient. But everyone is excited and watches the progress. Mr. Stuben from the third floor comes up every morning before he leaves for work. Every day he says, 'Mikhail, you have your work cut out for you.'" He grinned as he opened the door. "Some days I'd like to throw my hammer at him." He stepped back and nudged her inside. "Sit."

Lips pursed, Sydney studied the room. The furniture had been pushed together in the center—to make it easier to work, she imagined. Tables were stacked on top of chairs, the rug had been rolled up. Under the sheet he'd tossed over his worktable were a variety of interesting shapes that were his sculptures, his tools, and blocks of wood yet to be carved.

It smelled like sawdust, she thought, and turpentine.

"Where?"

He stopped on his way to the kitchen and looked back. After a quick study, he leaned into the jumble and lifted out an old oak rocker. One-handed, Sydney noted, and felt foolish and impressed.

"Here." After setting it on a clear spot, he headed back into the kitchen.

The surface of the rocker was smooth as satin. When Sydney sat, she found the chair slipped around her like comforting arms. Ten seconds after she'd settled, she was moving it gently to and fro.

"This is beautiful."

He could hear the faint creak as the rocker moved and didn't bother to turn. "I made it for my sister years ago when she had a baby." His voice changed subtly as he turned on the kitchen tap. "She lost the baby, Lily, after only a few months, and it was painful for Natasha to keep the chair."

"I'm sorry." The creaking stopped. "I can't think of anything worse for a parent to face."

"Because there is nothing." He came back in, carrying a glass of water and a bottle. "Lily will always leave a little scar on the heart. But Tash has three children now. So pain is balanced with joy. Here." He put the glass in her hand, then shook two aspirin out of the bottle. "You have a headache."

She frowned down at the pills he dropped into her palm. True, her head was splitting, but she hadn't mentioned it. "I might have a little one," she muttered. "How do you know?"

"I can see it in your eyes." He waited until she'd sipped and swallowed, then walked behind the chair to circle her temples with his fingers. "It's not such a little one, either."

There was no doubt she should tell him to stop. And she would. Any minute. Unable to resist, she leaned back, letting her eyes close as his fingers stroked away the worst of the pain.

"Is this what you had for me? Headache remedies?"

Her voice was so quiet, so tired that his heart twisted a little. "No, I have something else for you. But it can wait until you're feeling better. Talk to me, Sydney. Tell me what's wrong. Maybe I can help."

"It's something I have to take care of myself."

"Okay. Will that change if you talk to me?"

No, she thought. It was her problem, her future. But what harm would it do to talk it out, to say it all out loud and hear someone else's viewpoint?

"Office politics." She sighed as he began to massage the base of her neck. His rough, calloused fingers were as gentle as a mother's. "I imagine they can be tricky enough when you have experience. All I have is the family name and my grandfather's last wishes. The publicity on Mrs. Wolburg has left my position in the company very shaky. I assumed responsibility without going through channels or consulting legal. The board isn't pleased with me."

His eyes had darkened, but his hands remained gentle. "Because you have integrity?"

"Because I jumped the gun, so to speak. The resulting publicity only made things worse. The consensus is that someone with more savvy could have handled the Wolburg matter—that's how it's referred to at Hayward. The Wolburg matter in a quiet, tidy fashion. There's a board meeting at noon on Friday, and they could very well request that I step down as president."

"And will you?"

"I don't know." He was working on her shoulders now, competently, thoroughly. "I'd like to fight, draw the whole thing out. Then again, the company's been in upheaval for over a year, and having the president and the board as adversaries won't help Hayward. Added to that, my executive vice president and I are already on poor terms. He feels, perhaps justifiably, that he should be in the number one slot." She laughed softly. "There are times I wish he had it."

"No, you don't." He resisted the urge to bend down and press his lips to the long, slender column of her neck. Barely. "You like being in charge, and I think you're good at it."

She stopped rocking to turn her head and stare at him. "You're the first person who's ever said that to me. Most of the people who know me think I'm playing at this, or that I'm experiencing a kind of temporary insanity."

His hand slid lightly down her arm as he came around to crouch in front of her. "Then they don't know you, do they?"

There were so many emotions popping through her as she kept her eyes on his. But pleasure, the simple pleasure of being understood was paramount.

"Maybe they don't," she murmured. "Maybe they don't."

"I won't give you advice." He picked up one of her hands because he enjoyed examining it, the long, ringless fingers, the slender wrist, the smooth, cool skin. "I don't know about office politics or board meetings. But I think you'll do what's right. You have a good brain and a good heart."

Hardly aware that she'd turned her hand over under his and linked them, she smiled. The connection was more complete than joined fingers, and she couldn't understand it. This was support, a belief in her, and an encouragement she'd never expected to find.

"Odd that I'd have to come to a Ukrainian carpenter for a pep talk. Thanks."

"You're welcome." He looked back into her eyes. "Your headache's gone."

Surprised, she touched her fingers to her temple. "Yes, yes it is." In fact, she couldn't remember ever feeling more relaxed. "You could make a fortune with those hands."

He grinned and slid them up her arms, pushing the sleeves of her jacket along so he could feel the bare flesh beneath. "It's only a matter of knowing what to do with them, and when." And he knew exactly how he wanted to use those hands on her. Unfortunately, the timing was wrong.

"Yes, well . . ." It was happening again, those little licks of fire in the pit of her stomach, the trembling heat along her skin. "I really am grateful, for everything. I should be going."

"You have time yet." His fingers glided back down her arms to link with hers. "I haven't given you your present."

"Present?" He was drawing her slowly to her feet. Now they were thigh to thigh, her eyes level with his mouth. It was curved and close, sending her system into overdrive.

He had only to lean down. Inches, bare inches. Imagining it nearly drove him crazy. Not an altogether unpleasant feeling, he discovered, this anticipation, this wondering. If she offered, and only when she offered, would he take.

"Don't you like presents, *milaya?*"

His voice was like hot cream, pouring richly over her. "I...the report," she said, remembering. "Weren't you going to give me your report?"

His thumbs skimmed over her wrist and felt the erratic beat of her pulse. It was tempting, very tempting. "I can send the report. I had something else in mind."

"Something..." Her own mind quite simply shut down.

He laughed, so delighted with her he wanted to kiss her breathless. Instead he released her hands and walked away. She didn't move, not an inch as he strolled over to the shelves and tossed up the drop cloth. In a moment he was back, pressing the little Cinderella into her hand.

"I'd like you to have this."

"Oh, but..." She tried, really tried to form a proper refusal. The words wouldn't come.

"You don't like?"

"No. I mean, yes, of course I like it, it's exquisite. But why?" Her fingers were already curving possessively around it when she lifted her eyes to his. "Why would you give it to me?"

"Because she reminds me of you. She's lovely, fragile, unsure of herself."

The description had Sydney's pleasure dimming. "Most people would term her romantic."

"I'm not most. Here, as she runs away, she doesn't believe enough." He stroked a finger down the delicate folds of the ball gown. "She follows the rules, without question. It's midnight, and she was in the arms of her prince, but she breaks away and runs. Because that was the rule. And she is afraid, afraid to let him see beneath the illusion to the woman."

"She had to leave. She'd promised. Besides, she'd have been humiliated to have been caught there in rags and bare feet."

Tilting his head, Mikhail studied her. "Do you think he cared about her dress?"

"Well, no, I don't suppose it would have mattered to him." Sydney let out an impatient breath as he grinned at her. It was ridiculous, standing here debating the psychology of a fairy-tale character. "In any case, it ended happily, and though I've nothing in common with Cinderella, the figurine's beautiful. I'll treasure it."

"Good. Now, I'll walk you downstairs. You don't want to be late for dinner with your mother."

"She won't be there until eight-thirty. She's always late." Halfway through the door, Sydney stopped. "How did you know I was meeting my mother?"

"She told me, ah, two days ago. We had a drink uptown."

Sydney turned completely around so that he was standing on one side of the threshold, she on the other. "You had drinks with my mother?" she asked, spacing each word carefully.

"Yes." Lazily he leaned on the jamb. "Before you try to turn me into an iceberg, understand that I have no sexual interest in Margerite."

"That's lovely. Just lovely." If she hadn't already put the figurine into her purse, she might have thrown it in his face. "We agreed you'd leave my mother alone."

"We agreed nothing," he corrected. "And I don't bother your mother." There was little to be gained by telling her that Margerite had called him three times before he'd given in and met her. "It was a friendly drink, and after it was done, I think Margerite understood we are unsuitable for anything but friendship. Particularly," he said, holding up a finger to block her interruption, "since I am very sexually interested in her daughter."

That stopped her words cold. She swallowed, struggled for composure and failed. "You are not, all you're interested in is scoring a few macho points."

Something flickered in his eyes. "Would you like to come back inside so that I can show you exactly what I'm interested in?"

"No." Before she could stop herself, she'd taken a retreating step. "But I would like you to have the decency not to play games with my mother."

He wondered if Margerite would leap so quickly to her daughter's defense, or if Sydney would understand that her mother was only interested in a brief affair with a younger man—something he'd made very clear he wanted no part in.

"Since I would hate for your headache to come back after I went to the trouble to rid you of it, I will make myself as clear as I can. I have no intention of becoming romantically, physically or emotionally involved with your mother. Does that suit you?"

"It would if I could believe you."

He didn't move, not a muscle, but she sensed he had cocked, like the hammer on a gun. His voice was low and deadly. "I don't lie."

She nodded, cool as an ice slick. "Just stick to hammering nails, Mikhail. We'll get along fine. And I can find my own way down." She didn't whirl away, but turned slowly and walked to the elevator. Though she didn't look back as she stepped inside, she was well aware that he watched her go.

At noon sharp, Sydney sat at the head of the long walnut table of the boardroom. Ten men and two women were ranged down either side with crystal tumblers at their elbows, pads and pens at the ready. Heavy brocade drapes were drawn back to reveal a wall of window, tinted to cut the glare of sunlight— had there been any. Instead there was a thick curtain of rain, gray as soot. She could just make out the silhouette of the Times Building. Occasionally a murmur of thunder sneaked in through the stone and glass.

The gloom suited her. Sydney felt exactly like the reckless child summoned to the principal's office.

She scanned the rows of faces, some of whom had belonged in this office, at this very table, since before she'd been born. Perhaps they would be the toughest to sway, those who thought of her as the little girl who had come to Hayward to bounce on Grandfather's knee.

Then there was Lloyd, halfway down the gleaming surface, his face so smug, so confident, she wanted to snarl. No, she realized as his gaze flicked to hers and held. She wanted to win.

"Ladies, gentlemen." The moment the meeting was called to order she rose. "Before we begin discussion of the matter so much on our minds, I'd like to make a statement."

"You've already made your statement to the press, Sydney," Lloyd pointed out. "I believe everyone here is aware of your position."

There was a rippling murmur, some agreement, some dissent. She let it fade before she spoke again. "Nonetheless, as the president, and the major stockholder of Hayward, I will have my say, then the meeting will open for discussion."

Her throat froze as all eyes fixed on her. Some were patient, some indulgent, some speculative.

"I understand the board's unease with the amount of money allocated to the Soho project. Of Hayward's holdings, this building represents a relatively small annual income. However, this small income has been steady. Over the last ten years, this complex has needed—or I should say received—little or no maintenance. You know, of course, from the quarterly reports just how much this property has increased in value in this space of time. I believe, from a purely practical standpoint, that the money I allocated is insurance to protect our investment.''

She wanted to stop, to pick up her glass and drain it, but knew the gesture would make her seem as nervous as she was.

''In addition, I believe Hayward has a moral, an ethical and a legal obligation to insure that our tenants receive safe and decent housing.''

''That property could have been made safe and decent for half of the money budgeted,'' Lloyd put in.

Sydney barely glanced at him. ''You're quite right. I believe my grandfather wanted more than the minimum required for Hayward. He wanted it to be the best, the finest. I know I do. I won't stand here and quote you figures. They're in your folders and can be discussed at length in a few moments. Yes, the budget for the Soho project is high, and so are Hayward standards.''

''Sydney.'' Howard Keller, one of her grandfather's oldest associates spoke gently. ''None of us here doubt your motives or your enthusiasm. Your judgment, however, in this, and in the Wolburg matter, is something we must consider. The publicity over the past few days has been extremely detrimental. Hayward stock is down a full three percent. That's in addition to the drop we suffered when you took your position as head of the company. Our stockholders are, understandably, concerned.''

''The Wolburg matter,'' Sydney said with steel in her voice, ''is an eighty-year-old woman with a fractured hip. She fell because the floor in her kitchen, a floor we neglected to replace, was unsafe.''

"It's precisely that kind of reckless statement that will open Hayward up to a major lawsuit," Lloyd put in. He kept his tone the quiet sound of calm reason. "Isn't it the function of insurance investigators and legal to come to a decision on this, after a careful, thoughtful overview of the situation? We can't run our company on emotion and impulse. Miss Hayward's heart might have been touched by the Wolburg matter, but there are procedures, channels to be used. Now that the press has jumped on this—"

"Yes," she broke in. "It's very interesting how quickly the press learned about the accident. It's hard to believe that only days after an unknown, unimportant old lady falls in her downtown apartment, the press is slapping Hayward in the headlines."

"I would imagine she called them herself," Lloyd said.

Her smile was icy. "Would you?"

"I don't think the issue is how the press got wind of this," Mavis Trelane commented. "The point is they did, and the resulting publicity has been shaded heavily against us, putting Hayward in a very vulnerable position. The stockholders want a solution quickly."

"Does anyone here believe Hayward is not culpable for Mrs. Wolburg's injuries?"

"It's not what we believe," Mavis corrected. "And none of us could make a decision on that until a full investigation into the incident. What is relevant is how such matters are handled."

She frowned when a knock interrupted her.

"I'm sorry," Sydney said, and moved away from the table to walk stiffly to the door. "Janine, I explained we weren't to be interrupted."

"Yes, ma'am." The secretary, who had thrown her loyalty to Sydney five minutes after hearing the story, kept her voice low. "This is important. I just got a call from a friend of mine. He works on Channel 6. Mrs. Wolburg's going to make a statement on the Noon News. Any minute now."

After a moment's hesitation, Sydney nodded. "Thank you, Janine."

"Good luck, Ms. Hayward."

Sydney smiled and shut the door. She was going to need it. Face composed, she turned back to the room. "I've just been told that Mrs. Wolburg is about to make a televised statement. I'm sure we're all interested in what she has to say. So with your permission, I'll turn on the set." Rather than waiting for the debate to settle it, Sydney picked up the remote and aimed it at the console in the corner.

While Lloyd was stating that the board needed to concern themselves with the facts and not a publicity maneuver, Channel 6 cut from commercial to Mrs. Wolburg's hospital bed.

The reporter, a pretty woman in her early twenties with eyes as sharp as nails, began the interview by asking the patient to explain how she came by her injury.

Several members of the board shook their heads and muttered among themselves as she explained about tripping on the ripped linoleum and how the noise of the construction had masked her calls for help.

Lloyd had to stop his lips from curving as he imagined Sydney's ship springing another leak.

"And this floor," the reporter continued. "Had the condition of it been reported to Hayward?"

"Oh, sure. Mik—that's Mikhail Stanislaski, the sweet boy up on the fifth floor wrote letters about the whole building."

"And nothing was done?"

"Nope, not a thing. Why Mr. and Mrs. Kowalski, the young couple in 101, had a piece of plaster as big as a pie plate fall out of their ceiling. Mik fixed it."

"So the tenants were forced to take on the repairs themselves, due to Hayward's neglect."

"I guess you could say that. Up until the last few weeks."

"Oh, and what happened in the last few weeks?"

"That would be when Sydney—that's Miss Hayward—took over the company. She's the granddaughter of old man Hayward. Heard he'd been real sick the last couple years. Guess things got away from him. Anyway, Mik went to see her, and she came out herself that very day to take a look. Not two weeks later, and the building was crawling with construction workers. We got new windows. Got a new roof going on right this minute. All the plumbing's being fixed, too. Every single thing Mik put on the list is going to be taken care of."

"Really? And did all this happen before or after your injury?"

"Before," Mrs. Wolburg said, a bit impatient with the sarcasm. "I told you all that hammering and sawing was the reason nobody heard me when I fell. And I want you to know that Miss Hayward was there checking the place out again that day. She and Mik found me. She sat right there on the floor and talked to me, brought me a pillow and a blanket and stayed with me until the ambulance came. Came to the hospital, too, and took care of all my medical bills. Been to visit me three times since I've been here.''

''Wouldn't you say that Hayward, and therefore Sydney Hayward, is responsible for you being here?''

''Bad eyes and a hole in the floor's responsible,'' she said evenly. ''And I'll tell you just what I told those ambulance chasers who've been calling my family. I've got no reason to sue Hayward. They've been taking care of me since the minute I was hurt. Now maybe if they'd dallied around and tried to make like it wasn't any of their doing, I'd feel differently. But they did what was right, and you can't ask for better than that. Sydney's got ethics, and as long as she's in charge I figure Hayward has ethics, too. I'm pleased to live in a building owned by a company with a conscience.''

Sydney stayed where she was after the interview ended. Saying nothing, she switched off the set and waited.

''You can't buy that kind of goodwill,'' Mavis decided. ''Your method may have been unorthodox, Sydney, and I don't doubt there will still be some backwash to deal with, but all in all, I think the stockholders will be pleased.''

The discussion labored on another thirty minutes, but the crisis had passed.

The moment Sydney was back in her own office, she picked up the phone. The receiver rang in her ear twelve times, frustrating her, before it was finally picked up on the other end.

''Yeah?''

''Mikhail?''

''Nope, he's down the hall.''

"Oh, well then, I—"

"Hang on." The phone rattled, clanged then clattered as the male voice boomed out Mikhail's name. Feeling like a fool, Sydney stayed on the line.

"Hello?"

"Mikhail, it's Sydney."

He grinned and grabbed the jug of ice water out of the refrigerator. "Hello, anyway."

"I just saw the news. I suppose you knew."

"Caught it on my lunch break. So?"

"You asked her to do it?"

"No, I didn't." He paused long enough to gulp down about a pint of water. "I told her how things were, and she came up with the idea herself. It was a good one."

"Yes, it was a good one. And I owe you."

"Yeah?" He thought about it. "Okay. Pay up."

Why she'd expected him to politely refuse to take credit was beyond her. "Excuse me?"

"Pay up, Hayward. You can have dinner with me on Sunday."

"Really, I don't see how one has to do with the other."

"You owe me," he reminded her, "and that's what I want. Nothing fancy, okay? I'll pick you up around four."

"Four? Four in the afternoon for dinner?"

"Right." He pulled a carpenter's pencil out of his pocket. "What's your address?"

He let out a low whistle as she reluctantly rattled it off. "Nice." He finished writing it on the wall. "Got a phone number? In case something comes up."

She was scowling, but she gave it to him. "I want to make it clear that—"

"Make it clear when I pick you up. I'm on the clock, and you're paying." On impulse he outlined her address and phone number with a heart. "See you Sunday. Boss."

Chapter Six

Sydney studied her reflection in the cheval glass critically and cautiously. It wasn't as if it were a date. She'd reminded herself of that several hundred times over the weekend. It was more of a payment, and no matter how she felt about Mikhail, she owed him. Haywards paid their debts.

Nothing formal. She'd taken him at his word there. The little dress was simple, its scooped neck and thin straps a concession to the heat. The nipped in waist was flattering, the flared skirt comfortable. The thin, nearly weightless material was teal blue. Not that she'd paid any attention to his suggestion she wear brighter colors.

Maybe the dress was new, purchased after a frantic two hours of searching—but that was only because she'd wanted something new.

The short gold chain with its tiny links and the hoops at her ears were plain but elegant. She'd spent longer than usual on her makeup, but that was only because she'd been experimenting with some new shades of eyeshadow.

After much debate, she'd opted to leave her hair down. Then, of course, she'd had to fool with it until the style suited her. Fluffed out, skimming just above her shoulders seemed casual enough to her. And sexy. Not that she cared about being sexy tonight, but a woman was entitled to a certain amount of vanity.

She hesitated over the cut-glass decanter of perfume, remembering how Mikhail had described her scent. With a shrug, she touched it to pulse points. It hardly mattered if it appealed to him. She was wearing it for herself.

Satisfied, she checked the contents of her purse, then her watch. She was a full hour early. Blowing out a long breath, she sat down on the bed. For the first time in her life, she actively wished for a drink.

An hour and fifteen minutes later, after she had wandered through the apartment, plumping pillows, rearranging statuary then putting it back where it had been in the first place, he knocked on the door. She stopped in the foyer, found she had to fuss with her hair another moment, then pressed a hand to her nervous stomach. Outwardly composed, she opened the door.

It didn't appear he'd worried overmuch about his attire. The jeans were clean but faded, the high-tops only slightly less scuffed than his usual work boots. His shirt was tucked in—a definite change—and was a plain, working man's cotton the color of smoke. His hair flowed over the collar, so black, so untamed no woman alive could help but fantasize about letting her fingers dive in.

He looked earthy, a little wild, and more than a little dangerous.

And he'd brought her a tulip.

"I'm late." He held out the flower, thinking she looked as cool and delicious as a sherbert parfait in a crystal dish. "I was working on your face."

"You were—what?"

"Your face." He slid a hand under her chin, his eyes narrowing in concentration. "I found the right piece of rosewood and lost track of time." As he studied, his fingers moved over her face as they had the wood, searching for answers. "You will ask me in?"

Her mind, empty as a leaky bucket, struggled to fill again. "Of course. For a minute." She stepped back, breaking contact. "I'll just put this in water."

When she left him, Mikhail let his gaze sweep the room. It pleased him. This was not the formal, professionally decorated home some might have expected of her. She really lived here, among the soft colors and quiet comfort. Style was added by a scattering of Art Nouveau, in the bronzed lamp shaped like a long, slim woman, and the sinuous etched flowers on the glass doors of a curio cabinet displaying a collection of antique beaded bags.

He noted his sculpture stood alone in a glossy old shadow box, and was flattered.

She came back, carrying the tulip in a slim silver vase.

"I admire your taste."

She set the vase atop the curio. "Thank you."

"Nouveau is sensuous." He traced a finger down the flowing lines of the lamp. "And rebellious."

She nearly frowned before she caught herself. "I find it attractive. Graceful."

"Graceful, yes. Also powerful."

She didn't care for the way he was smiling at her, as if he knew a secret she didn't. And that the secret was her. "Yes, well, I'm sure as an artist you'd agree art should have power. Would you like a drink before we go?"

"No, not before I drive."

"Drive?"

"Yes. Do you like Sunday drives, Sydney?"

"I..." She picked up her purse to give her hands something to do. There was no reason, none at all, for her to allow him to make her feel as awkward as a teenager on a first date. "I don't get much opportunity for them in the city." It seemed wise to get started. She moved to the door, wondering what it would be like to be in a car with him. Alone. "I didn't realize you kept a car."

His grin was quick and a tad self-mocking as they moved out into the hall. "A couple of years ago, after my art had some success, I bought one. It was a little fantasy of mine. I think I pay more to keep it parked than I did for the car. But fantasies are rarely free."

In the elevator, he pushed the button for the garage. "I think about it myself," she admitted. "I miss driving, the independence of it, I suppose. In Europe, I could hop in and zoom off whenever I chose. But it seems more practical to keep a driver here than to go to war every time you need a parking space."

"Sometime we'll go up north, along the river, and you can drive."

The image was almost too appealing, whipping along the roads toward the mountains upstate. She thought it was best not to comment. "Your report came in on Friday," she began.

"Not today." He reached down to take her hand as they stepped into the echoing garage. "Talking reports can wait till Monday. Here." He opened the door of a glossy red-and-cream MG. The canvas top was lowered. "You don't mind the top down?" he asked as she settled inside.

Sydney thought of the time and trouble she'd taken with her hair. And she thought of the freedom of having even a hot breeze blow through it. "No, I don't mind."

He climbed into the driver's seat, adjusting long legs, then gunned the engine. After taking a pair of mirrored sunglasses off the dash, he pulled out. The radio was set on rock. Sydney found herself smiling as they cruised around Central Park.

"You didn't mention where we were going."

"I know this little place. The food is good." He noted her foot was tapping along in time with the music. "Tell me where you lived in Europe."

"Oh, I didn't live in any one place. I moved around. Paris, Saint Tropez, Venice, London, Monte Carlo."

"Perhaps you have Gypsies in your blood, too."

"Perhaps." Not Gypsies, she thought. There had been nothing so romantic as wanderlust in her hopscotching travels through Europe. Only dissatisfaction, and a need to hide until wounds had healed. "Have you ever been?"

"When I was very young. But I would like to go back now that I am old enough to appreciate it. The art, you see, and the atmosphere, the architecture. What places did you like best?"

"A little village in the countryside of France where they milked cows by hand and grew fat purple grapes. There was a courtyard at the inn where I stayed, and the flowers were so big and bright. In the late afternoon you could sit and drink the most wonderful white wine and listen to the doves coo." She stopped, faintly embarrassed. "And of course, Paris," she said quickly. "The food, the shopping, the ballet. I knew several people, and enjoyed the parties."

Not so much, he thought, as she enjoyed sitting alone and listening to cooing doves.

"Do you ever think about going back to the Soviet Union?" she asked him.

"Often. To see the place where I was born, the house we lived in. It may not be there now. The hills where I played as a child. They would be."

His glasses only tossed her own reflection back at her. But she thought, behind them, his eyes would be sad. His voice was. "Things have changed so much, so quickly in the last few years. Glasnost, the Berlin Wall. You could go back."

"Sometimes I think I will, then I wonder if it's better to leave it a memory—part bitter, part sweet, but colored through the eyes of a child. I was very young when we left."

"It was difficult."

"Yes. More for my parents who knew the risks better than we. They had the courage to give up everything they had ever known to give their children the one thing they had never had. Freedom."

Moved, she laid a hand over his on the gearshift. Margerite had told her the story of escaping into Hungary in a wagon, making it seem like some sort of romantic adventure. It didn't seem romantic to Sydney. It seemed terrifying. "You must have been frightened."

"More than I ever hope to be again. At night I would lie awake, always cold, always hungry, and listen to my parents talk. One would reassure the other, and they would plan how far we might travel the next day—and the next. When we came to America, my father wept. And I understood it was over. I wasn't afraid anymore."

Her own eyes had filled. She turned away to let the wind dry them. "But coming here must have been frightening, too. A different place, different language, different culture."

He heard the emotion in her voice. Though touched, he didn't want to make her sad. Not today. "The young adjust quickly. I had only to give the boy in the next house a bloody nose to feel at home."

She turned back, saw the grin and responded with a laugh. "Then, I suppose, you became inseparable friends."

"I was best man at his wedding only two years ago."

With a shake of her head, she settled back. It was then she noticed they were crossing the bridge over to Brooklyn. "You couldn't find a place to have dinner in Manhattan?"

His grin widened. "Not like this one."

A few minutes later, he was cruising through one of the old neighborhoods with its faded brick row houses and big, shady trees. Children scrambled along the sidewalks, riding bikes, jumping rope. At the curb where Mikhail stopped, two boys were having a deep and serious transaction with baseball cards.

"Hey, Mik!" Both of them jumped up before he'd even climbed out of the car. "You missed the game. We finished an hour ago."

"I'll catch the next one." He glanced over to see that Sydney had already gotten out and was standing in the street, studying the neighborhood with baffled and wary eyes. He leaned over and winked. "I got a hot date."

"Oh, man." Twelve-year-old disgust prevented either of them from further comment.

Laughing, Mikhail walked over to grab Sydney's hand and pull her to the sidewalk. "I don't understand," she began as he led her across the concrete heaved up by the roots of a huge old oak. "This is a restaurant?"

"No." He had to tug to make her keep up with him as he climbed the steps. "It's a house."

"But you said—"

"That we were going to dinner." He shoved the door open and took a deep sniff. "Smells like Mama made Chicken Kiev. You'll like."

"Your mother?" She nearly stumbled into the narrow entrance way. Scattered emotions flew inside her stomach like a bevy of birds. "You bought me to your parents' house?"

"Yes, for Sunday dinner."

"Oh, good Lord."

He lifted a brow. "You don't like Chicken Kiev?"

"No. Yes. That isn't the point. I wasn't expecting—"

"You're late," Yuri boomed. "Are you going to bring the woman in or stand in the doorway?"

Mikhail kept his eyes on Sydney's. "She doesn't want to come in," he called back.

"That's not it," she whispered, mortified. "You might have told me about this so I could have...oh, never mind." She brushed past him to take the couple of steps necessary to bring her into the living room. Yuri was just hauling himself out of a chair.

"Mr. Stanislaski, it's so nice of you to have me." She offered a hand and had it swallowed whole by his.

"You are welcome here. You will call me Yuri."

"Thank you."

"We are happy Mikhail shows good taste." Grinning, he used a stage whisper. "His mama, she didn't like the dancer with the blond hair."

"Thanks, Papa." Casually Mikhail draped an arm over Sydney's shoulders—felt her resist the urge to shrug it off. "Where is everyone?"

"Mama and Rachel are in the kitchen. Alex is later than you. Alex sees all the girls, at the same time," Yuri told Sydney. "It should confuse him, but it does not."

"Yuri, you have not taken the trash out yet." A small woman with an exotic face and graying hair came out of the kitchen, carrying silverware in the skirt of her apron.

Yuri gave his son an affectionate thump on the back that nearly had Sydney pitching forward. "I wait for Mikhail to come and take it."

"And Mikhail will wait for Alex." She set the flatware down on a heavy table at the other end of the room, then came to Sydney. Her dark eyes were shrewd, not unfriendly, but quietly probing. She smelled of spice and melted butter. "I am Nadia, Mikhail's mother." She offered a hand. "We are happy to have you with us."

"Thank you. You have a lovely home."

She had said it automatically, meaningless politeness. But the moment the words were out, Sydney realized they were true. The entire house would probably fit into one wing of her mother's Long Island estate, and the furniture was old rather than antique. Doilies as charming and intricate as those she had seen at Mrs. Wolburg's covered the arms of chairs. The wallpaper was faded, but that only made the tiny rosebuds scattered over it seem more lovely.

The strong sunlight burst through the window and showed every scar, every mend. Just as it showed how lovingly the woodwork and table surfaces had been polished.

Out of the corner of her eye she caught a movement. As she glanced over, she watched a plump ball of gray fur struggling, whimpering from under a chair.

"That is Ivan," Yuri said, clucking to the puppy. "He is only a baby." He sighed a little for his old mutt Sasha who had died peacefully at the age of fifteen six months before. "Alex brings him home from pound."

"Saved you from walking the last mile, right, Ivan?" Mikhail bent down to ruffle fur. Ivan thumped his tail while giving Sydney nervous looks. "He is named for Ivan the Terrible, but he's a coward."

"He's just shy," Sydney corrected, then gave in to need and crouched down. She'd always wanted a pet, but boarding schools didn't permit them. "There, aren't you sweet?" The dog trembled visibly for a moment when she stroked him, then began to lick the toes that peeked out through her sandals.

Mikhail began to think the pup had potential.

"What kind is he?" she asked.

"He is part Russian wolfhound," Yuri declared.

"With plenty of traveling salesmen thrown in." The voice came from the kitchen doorway. Sydney looked over her shoulder and saw a striking woman with a sleek cap of raven hair and tawny eyes. "I'm Mikhail's sister, Rachel. You must be Sydney."

"Yes, hello." Sydney straightened, and wondered what miracles in the gene pool had made all the Stanislaskis so blindingly beautiful.

"Dinner'll be ready in ten minutes." Rachel's voice carried only the faintest wisp of an accent and was as dark and smooth as black velvet. "Mikhail, you can set the table."

"I have to take out the trash," he told her, instantly choosing the lesser of two evils.

"I'll do it." Sydney's impulsive offer was greeted with casual acceptance. She was nearly finished when Alex, as dark, exotic and gorgeous as the rest of the family, strolled in.

"Sorry I'm late, Papa. Just finished a double shift. I barely had time to..." He trailed off when he spotted Sydney. His mouth curved and his eyes flickered with definite interest. "Now I'm really sorry I'm late. Hi."

"Hello." Her lips curved in response. That kind of romantic charm could have raised the blood pressure on a corpse. Providing it was female.

"Mine," Mikhail said mildly as he strolled back out of the kitchen.

Alex merely grinned and continued walking toward Sydney. He took her hand, kissed the knuckles. "Just so you know, of the two of us, I'm less moody and have a steadier job."

She had to laugh. "I'll certainly take that into account."

"He thinks he's a cop." Mikhail sent his brother an amused look. "Mama says to wash your hands. Dinner's ready."

Sydney was certain she'd never seen more food at one table. There were mounds of chicken stuffed with rich, herbed butter. It was served with an enormous bowl of lightly browned potatoes and a platter heaped with slices of grilled vegetables that Nadia had picked from her own kitchen garden that morning. There was a tower of biscuits along with a mountain of some flaky stuffed pastries that was Alex's favorite dish.

Sydney sipped the crisp wine that was offered along with vodka and wondered. The amount and variety of food was nothing compared to the conversation.

Rachel and Alex argued over someone named Goose. After a winding explanation, Sydney learned that while Alex was a rookie cop, Rachel was in her first year with the public defender's office. And Goose was a petty thief Rachel was defending.

Yuri and Mikhail argued about baseball. Sydney didn't need Nadia's affectionate translation to realize that while Yuri was a diehard Yankee fan, Mikhail stood behind the Mets.

There was much gesturing with silverware and Russian exclamations mixed with English. Then laughter, a shouted question, and more arguing.

"Rachel is an idealist," Alex stated. With his elbows on the table and his chin rested on his joined hands, he smiled at Sydney. "What are you?"

She smiled back. "Too smart to be put between a lawyer and a cop."

"Elbows off," Nadia said, and gave her son a quick rap. "Mikhail says you are a businesswoman. And that you are very smart. And fair."

The description surprised her enough that she nearly fumbled. "I try to be."

"Your company was in a sticky situation last week." Rachel downed the last of her vodka with a panache Sydney admired. "You handled it well. It seemed to me that rather than trying to be fair you simply were. Have you known Mikhail long?"

She segued into the question so neatly, Sydney only blinked. "No, actually. We met last month when he barged into my office ready to crush any available Hayward under his work boot."

"I was polite," he corrected.

"You were not polite." Because she could see Yuri was amused, she continued. "He was dirty, angry and ready to fight."

"His temper comes from his mama," Yuri informed Sydney. "She is fierce."

"Only once," Nadia said with a shake of her head. "Only once did I hit him over the head with a pot. He never forgets."

"I still have the scar. And here." Yuri pointed to his shoulder. "Where you threw the hairbrush at me."

"You should not have said my new dress was ugly."

"It was ugly," he said with a shrug, then tapped a hand on his chest. "And here, where you—"

"Enough." All dignity, she rose. "Or our guest will think I am tyrant."

"She is a tyrant," Yuri told Sydney with a grin.

"And this tyrant says we will clear the table and have dessert."

Sydney was still chuckling over it as Mikhail crossed the bridge back into Manhattan. Sometime during the long, comfortable meal she'd forgotten to be annoyed with him. Perhaps she'd had a half a glass too much wine. Certainly she'd eaten entirely too much kissel—the heavenly apricot pudding Nadia had served with cold, rich cream. But she was relaxed and couldn't remember ever having spent a more enjoyable Sunday evening.

"Did your father make that up?" Snuggled back in her seat, Sydney turned her head to study Mikhail's profile. "About your mother throwing things?"

"No, she throws things." He downshifted and cruised into traffic. "Once a whole plate of spaghetti and meatballs at me because my mouth was too quick."

Her laughter came out in a burst of enjoyment. "Oh, I would have loved to have seen that. Did you duck?"

He flicked her a grin. "Not fast enough."

"I've never thrown anything in my life." Her sigh was part wistful, part envious. "I think it must be very liberating. They're wonderful," she said after another moment. "Your family. You're very lucky."

"So you don't mind eating in Brooklyn?"

Frowning, she straightened a bit. "It wasn't that. I told you, I'm not a snob. I just wasn't prepared. You should have told me you were taking me there."

"Would you have gone?"

She opened her mouth then closed it again. After a moment, she let her shoulders rise and fall. "I don't know. Why did you take me?"

"I wanted to see you there. Maybe I wanted you to see me there, too."

Puzzled, she turned to look at him again. They were nearly back now. In a few more minutes he would go his way and she hers. "I don't understand why that should matter to you."

"Then you understand much too little, Sydney."

"I might understand if you'd be more clear." It was suddenly important, vital, that she know. The tips of her fingers were beginning to tingle so that she had to rub them together to stop the sensation.

"I'm better with my hands than with words." Impatient with her, with himself, he pulled into the garage beneath her building. When he yanked off his sunglasses, his eyes were dark and turbulent.

Didn't she know that her damn perfume had his nerve ends sizzling? The way she laughed, the way her hair lifted in the wind. How her eyes had softened and yearned as she'd looked at the silly little mutt of his father's.

It was worse, much worse now that he'd seen her with his family. Now that he'd watched how her initial stiffness melted away under a few kind words. He'd worried that he'd made a mistake, that she would be cold to his family, disdainful of the old house and simple meal.

Instead she'd laughed with his father, dried dishes with his mother. Alex's blatant flirting hadn't offended but rather had amused her. And when Rachel had praised her handling of the accident with Mrs. Wolburg, she'd flushed like a schoolgirl.

How the hell was he supposed to know he'd fall in love with her?

And now that she was alone with him again, all that cool reserve was seeping back. He could see it in the way her spine straightened when she stepped out of the car.

Hell, he could feel it—it surprised him that frost didn't form on his windshield.

"I'll walk you up." He slammed the door of the car.

"That isn't necessary." She didn't know what had spoiled the evening, but was ready to place the blame squarely on his shoulders.

"I'll walk you up," he repeated, and pulled her over to the elevator.

"Fine." She folded her arms and waited.

The moment the doors opened, they entered without speaking. Both of them were sure it was the longest elevator ride on record. Sydney swept out in front of him when they reached her floor. She had her keys out and ready two steps before they hit her door.

"I enjoyed your family," she said, carefully polite. "Be sure to tell your parents again how much I appreciated their hospitality." The lock snapped open.

"You can reach me in the office if there are any problems this week."

He slapped his hand on the door before she could shut it in his face. "I'm coming in."

Chapter Seven

Sydney considered the chances of shoving the door closed while he had his weight against it, found them slim and opted for shivery reserve.

"It's a bit early for a nightcap and a bit late for coffee."

"I don't want a drink." Mikhail rapped the door closed with enough force to make the foyer mirror rattle.

Though she refused to back up, Sydney felt her stomach muscles experience the same helpless shaking. "Some people might consider it poor manners for a man to bully his way into a woman's apartment."

"I have poor manners," he told her, and, jamming his hands into his pockets, paced into the living room.

"It must be a trial for your parents. Obviously they worked hard to instill a certain code of behavior in their children. It didn't stick with you."

He swung back, and she was reminded of some compact and muscled cat on the prowl. Definitely a man-eater. "You liked them?"

Baffled, she pushed a hand through her disordered hair. "Of course I like them. I've already said so."

While his hands bunched and unbunched in his pockets, he lifted a brow. "I thought perhaps it was just your very perfect manners that made you say so."

As an insult, it was a well-aimed shot. Indignation shivered through the ice. "Well, you were wrong. Now if we've settled everything, you can go."

"We've settled nothing. You tell me why you are so different now from the way you were an hour ago."

She caught herself, tightening her lips before they could move into a pout. "I don't know what you're talking about."

"With my family you were warm and sweet. You smiled so easily. Now with me, you're cold and far away. You don't smile at all."

"That's absurd." Though it was little more than a baring of teeth, she forced her lips to curve. "There, I've smiled at you. Satisfied?"

Temper flickered into his eyes as he began to pace again. "I haven't been satisfied since I walk into your office. You make me suffer and I don't like it."

"Artists are supposed to suffer," she shot back. "And I don't see how I've had anything to do with it. I've given in to every single demand you made. Replaced windows, ripped out plumbing, gotten rid of that tool-and-knot wiring."

"Tube and knob," he corrected, nearly amused.

"Well, it's gone, isn't it? Have you any idea just how much lumber I've authorized?"

"To last two-by-four, I know. This is not point."

She studied him owlishly. "Do you know you drop your articles when you're angry?"

His eyes narrowed. "I drop nothing."

"Your *the*'s and *an*'s and *a*'s," she pointed out. "And your sentence structure suffers. You mix your tenses."

That wounded. "I'd like to hear you speak my language."

She set the purse she still carried onto a table with a snap. "Baryshnikov, glasnost."

His lips curled. "This is Russian. I am Ukrainian. This is a mistake you make, but I overlook."

"It. You overlook *it*," she corrected. "In any case, it's close enough." He took a step forward, she took one back. "I'm sure we can have a fascinating discussion on the subtleties of language, but it will have to wait." He came closer, and she—casually, she hoped—edged away. "As I said before, I enjoyed the evening. Now—" he maneuvered her around a chair "—stop stalking me."

"You imagine things. You're not *a* rabbit, you're *a* woman."

But she felt like a rabbit, one of those poor, frozen creatures caught in a beam of headlights. "I don't know what's put you in this mood—"

"I have many moods. You put me in this one every time I see you, or think about you."

She shifted so that a table was between them. Because she well knew if she kept retreating her back would be against the wall, she took a stand. "All right, damn it. What do you want?"

"You. You know I want you."

Her heart leaped into her throat, then plummeted to her stomach. "You do not." The tremble in her voice irritated her enough to make her force ice into it. "I don't appreciate this game you're playing."

"I play? What is a man to think when a woman blows hot, then cold? When she looks at him with passion one minute and frost the next?" His hands lifted in frustration, then slapped down on the table. "I tell you straight out when you are so upset that I don't want your mama, I want you. And you call me a liar."

"I don't..." She could hardly get her breath. Deliberately she walked away, moving behind a chair and gripping the back hard. It had been a mistake to look into his eyes. There was a ruthlessness there that brought a terrible pitch of excitement to her blood. "You didn't want me before."

"Before? I think I wanted you before I met you. What is this before?"

"In the car." Humiliation washed her cheeks of color. "When I—when we were driving back from Long Island. We were..." Her fingers dug into the back of the chair. "It doesn't matter."

In two strides he was in front of the chair, his hands gripped over hers. "You tell me what you mean."

Pride, she told herself. She would damn well keep her pride. "All right then, to clarify, and to see that we don't have this conversation again. You started something in the car that night. I didn't ask for it, I didn't encourage it, but you started it." She took a deep breath to be certain her voice remained steady. "And you just stopped because...well, because I wasn't what you wanted after all."

For a moment he could only stare, too stunned for speech. Then his face changed, so quickly, Sydney could only blink at the surge of rage. When he acted, she gave a yip of surprise. The chair he yanked from between them landed on its side two feet away.

He swore at her. She didn't need to understand the words to appreciate the sentiment behind them. Before she could make an undignified retreat, his hands were clamped hard on her arms. For an instant she was afraid she was about to take the same flight as the chair. He was strong enough and certainly angry enough. But he only continued to shout.

It took her nearly a full minute to realize her feet were an inch above the floor and that he'd started using English again.

"Idiot. How can so smart a woman have no brains?"

"I'm not going to stand here and be insulted." Of course, she wasn't standing at all, she thought, fighting panic. She was dangling.

"It is not insult to speak truth. For weeks I have tried to be gentleman."

"*A* gentleman," she said furiously. "You've tried to be *a* gentleman. And you've failed miserably."

"I think you need time, you need me to show you how I feel. And I am sorry to have treated you as I did in the car that night. It makes me think you will have..." He trailed off, frustrated that the proper word wasn't in him. "That you will think me..."

"A heathen," she tossed out, with relish. "Barbarian."

"No, that's not so bad. But a man who abuses a woman for pleasure. Who forces and hurts her."

"It wasn't a matter of force," Sydney said coldly. "Now put me down."

He hiked her up another inch. "Do you think I stopped because I don't want you?"

"I'm well aware that my sexuality is under par."

He didn't have a clue what she was talking about, and plowed on. "We were in a car, in the middle of the city, with your driver in the front. And I was ready to rip your clothes away and take you, there. It made me angry with myself, and with you because you could make me forget."

She tried to think of a response. But he had set her back on her feet, and his hands were no longer gripping but caressing. The rage in his eyes had become something else, and it took her breath away.

"Every day since," he murmured. "Every night, I remember how you looked, how you felt. So I want more. And I wait for you to offer what I saw in your eyes that night. But you don't. I can't wait longer."

His fingers streaked into her hair, then fisted there, drawing her head back as his mouth crushed down on hers. The heat seered through her skin, into blood and bone. Her moan wasn't borne of pain but of tormented pleasure. Willing, desperately willing, her mouth parted under his, inviting him, accepting him. This time when her heart rose to her throat, there was a wild glory in it.

On an oath, he tore his mouth from hers and buried it against her throat. She had not asked, she had not encouraged. Those were her words, and he wouldn't ignore the truth of them. Whatever slippery grip he had on control, he clamped tight now, fighting to catch his breath and hold to sanity.

"Damn me to hell or take me to heaven," he muttered. "But do it now."

Her arms locked around his neck. He would leave, she knew, just as he had left that first time. And if he did she might never feel this frenzied stirring again. "I want you." *I'm afraid, I'm afraid.* "Yes, I want you. Make love to me."

And his mouth was on hers again, hard, hot, hungry, while his hands flowed like molten steel down her body. Not a caress now, but a branding. In one long, possessive stroke he staked a claim. It was too late for choices.

Fears and pleasures battered her, rough waves of emotion that had her trembling even as she absorbed delights. Her fingers dug into his shoulders, took greedy handfuls of his hair. Through the thin layers of cotton, she could feel the urgent drum of his heart and knew it beat for her.

More. He could only think he needed more, even as her scent swam in his head and her taste flooded his mouth. She moved against him, that small, slim body restless and eager. When he touched her, when his artist's hands sculpted her, finding the curves and planes of her already perfect, her low, throaty whimpers pounded in his ears like thunder.

More.

He tugged the straps from her shoulders, snapping one in his hurry to remove even that small obstacle. While his mouth raced over the smooth, bare curve, he dragged at the zipper, yanking and pulling until the dress pooled at her feet.

Beneath it. Oh, Lord, beneath it.

The strapless little fancy frothed over milk-white breasts, flowed down to long, lovely thighs. She lifted a trembling hand as if to cover herself, but he caught it, held it. He didn't see the nerves in her eyes as he filled himself on how she looked, surrounded in the last flames of sunset that warmed the room.

"Mikhail." Because he wasn't quite ready to speak, he only nodded. "I . . . the bedroom."

He'd been tempted to take her where they stood, or to do no more than drag her to the floor. Checking himself, he had her up in his arms in one glorious sweep. "It better be close."

On an unsteady laugh, she gestured. No man had ever carried her to bed before, and she found it dazzlingly romantic. Unsure of what part she should play, Sydney pressed her lips tentatively to his throat. He trembled. Encouraged, she skimmed them up to his ear. He groaned. On a sigh of pleasure, she continued to nibble while her fingers slipped beneath his shirt to stroke over his shoulder.

His arms tightened around her. When she turned her head, his mouth was there, taking greedily from hers as he tumbled with her onto the bed.

"Shouldn't we close the drapes?" The question ended on a gasp as he began doing things to her, wonderful things, shattering things. There was no room for shyness in this airless, spinning world.

It wasn't supposed to be like this. She'd always thought lovemaking to be either awkwardly mechanical or quietly comforting. It wasn't supposed to be so urgent, so turbulent. So incredible. Those rough, clever hands rushed over flesh, over silk, then back to flesh, leaving her a quivering mass of sensation. His mouth was just as hurried, just as skilled as it made the same erotic journey.

He was lost in her, utterly, irretrievably lost in her. Even the air was full of her, that quiet, restrained, gloriously seductive scent. Her skin seemed to melt, like liquid flowers, under his fingers, his lips. Each quick tremble he brought to her racked through him until he thought he would go mad.

Desire arced and spiked and hummed even as she grew softer, more pliant. More his.

Impatient, he brought his mouth to her breast to suckle through silk while his hands slid up her thighs to find her, wet and burning.

When he touched her, her body arched in shock. Her arm flew back until her fingers locked over one of the rungs of the brass headboard. She shook her head as pleasure shot into her, hot as a bullet. Suddenly fear and desire were so twisted into a single emotion she didn't know whether to beg him to stop or plead with him to go on. On and on.

Helpless, stripped of control, she gasped for breath. It seemed her system had contracted until she was curled into one tight hot ball. Even as she sobbed out his name, the ball imploded and she was left shattered.

A moan shuddered out as her body went limp again.

Unbearably aroused, he watched her, the stunned, glowing pleasure that flushed her cheeks, the dark, dazed desire that turned her eyes to blue smoke. For her, for himself, he took her up again, driving her higher until her breath was ragged and her body on fire.

"Please," she managed when he tugged the silk aside.

"I will please you." He flicked his tongue over her nipple. "And me."

There couldn't be more. But he showed her there was. Even when she began to drag frantically at his clothes, he continued to assault her system and to give her, give her more than she had ever believed she could hold. His hands were never still as he rolled over the bed with her, helping her to rid him of every possible barrier.

He wanted her crazed for him, as crazed as he for her. He could feel the wild need in the way she moved beneath him, in the way her hands searched. And yes, in the way she cried out when he found some secret she'd been keeping just for him.

When he could wait no longer, he plunged inside her, a sword to the hilt.

She was beyond pleasure. There was no name for the edge she trembled on. Her body moved, arching for his, finding their own intimate rhythm as naturally as breath. She knew he was speaking to her, desperate words in a mixture of languages. She understood that wherever she was, he was with her, as much a captive as she.

And when the power pushed her off that last thin edge, he was all there was. All there had to be.

It was dark, and the room was in shadows. Wondering if her mind would ever clear again, Sydney stared at the ceiling and listened to Mikhail breathe. It was foolish, she supposed, but it was such a soothing, intimate sound, that air moving quietly in and out of his lungs. She could have listened for hours.

Perhaps she had.

She had no idea how much time had passed since he'd slapped his hand on her door and barged in after her. It might have been minutes or hours, but it hardly mattered. Her life had been changed. Smiling to herself, she stroked a hand through his hair. He turned his head, just an inch, and pressed his lips to the underside of her jaw.

"I thought you were asleep," she murmured.

"No. I wouldn't fall asleep on top of you." He lifted his head. She could see the gleam of his eyes, the hint of a smile. "There are so many more interesting things to do on top of you."

She felt color rush to her cheeks and was grateful for the dark. "I was..." How could she ask? "It was all right, then?"

"No." Even with his body pressed into hers, he could feel her quick retreat. "Sydney, I may not have so many good words as you, but I think 'all right' is a poor choice. A walk through the park is all right."

"I only meant—" She shifted. Though he braced on his elbows to ease his weight from her, he made sure she couldn't wiggle away.

"I think we'll have a light now."

"No, that's not—" The bedside lamp clicked on. "Necessary."

"I want to see you, because I think I will make love with you again in a minute. And I like to look at you." Casually he brushed his lips over hers. "Don't."

"Don't what?"

"Tense your shoulders. I'd like to think you could relax with me."

"I am relaxed," she said, then blew out a long breath. No, she wasn't. "It's just that whenever I ask a direct question, you give evasions. I only wanted to know if you were, well, satisfied."

She'd been sure before, but now, as the heat had faded to warmth, she wondered if she'd only wished.

"Ah." Wrapping her close, he rolled over until she lay atop him. "This is like a quiz. Multiple choice. They were my favorite in school. You want to know, A, was it all right, B, was it very good or C, was it very wonderful."

"Forget it."

He clamped his arms around her when she tried to pull away. "I'm not finished with you, Hayward. I still have to answer the question, but I find there are not enough choices." He nudged her down until her lips had no choice but to meet his. And the kiss was long and sweet. "Do you understand now?"

His eyes were dark, still heavy from the pleasure they'd shared. The look in them said more than hundreds of silky words. "Yes."

"Good. Come back to me." He nestled her head on his shoulder and began to rub his hand gently up and down her back. "This is nice?"

"Yes." She smiled again. "This is nice." Moments passed in easy silence. "Mikhail."

"Hmm?"

"There weren't enough choices for me, either."

She was so beautiful when she slept, he could hardly look away. Her hair, a tangled flow of golden fire, curtained part of her face. One hand, small and delicate, curled on the pillow where his head had lain. The sheet, tangled from hours of loving showed the outline of her body to where the linen ended just at the curve of her breast.

She had been greater than any fantasy: generous, open, stunningly sexy and shy all at once. It had been like initiating a virgin and being seduced by a siren. And afterward, the faint embarrassment, the puzzling self-doubt. Where had that come from?

He would have to coax the answer from her. And if coaxing didn't work, he would bully.

But now, when he watched her in the morning light, he felt such an aching tenderness.

He hated to wake her, but he knew women enough to be sure she would be hurt if he left her sleeping.

Gently he brushed the hair from her cheek, bent down and kissed her.

She stirred and so did his desire.

He kissed her again, nibbling a trail to her ear. "Sydney." Her sleepy purr of response had his blood heating. "Wake up and kiss me goodbye."

"'S morning?" Her lashes fluttered up to reveal dark, heavy eyes. She stared at him a moment while she struggled to surface. His face was close and shadowed with stubble. To satisfy an old craving, she lifted her hand to it.

"You have a dangerous face." When he grinned, she propped herself up on an elbow. "You're dressed," she realized.

"I thought it the best way to go downtown."

"Go?"

Amused, he sat on the edge of the bed. "To work. It's nearly seven. I made coffee with your machine and used your shower."

She nodded. She could smell both—the coffee and the scent of her soap on his skin. "You should have waked me."

He twined a lock of her hair around his finger, enjoying the way its subtle fire seemed to lick at his flesh. "I didn't let you sleep very long last night. You will come downtown after work? I will fix you dinner."

Relieved, she smiled. "Yes."

"And you'll stay the night with me, sleep in my bed?"

She sat up so they were face-to-face. "Yes."

"Good." He tugged on the lock of hair. "Now kiss me goodbye."

"All right." Testing herself, she sat up, linked her hands around his neck. The sheet slid away to her waist. Pleased, she watched his gaze skim down, felt the tensing of muscles, saw the heat flash. Slowly, waiting until his eyes had come back to hers, she leaned forward. Her lips brushed his and retreated, brushed and retreated until she felt his quick groan. Satisfied she had his full attention, she flicked open the buttons of his shirt.

"Sydney." On a half laugh, he caught at her hands. "You'll make me late."

"That's the idea." She was smiling as she pushed the shirt off his shoulders. "Don't worry, I'll put in a good word for you with the boss."

Two hours later, Sydney strolled into her offices with an armful of flowers she'd bought on the street.

She'd left her hair down, had chosen a sunny yellow suit to match her mood. And she was humming.

Janine looked up from her work station, prepared to offer her usual morning greeting. The formal words stuck. "Wow. Ms. Hayward, you look fabulous."

"Thank you, Janine. I feel that way. These are for you."

Confused, Janine gathered up the armful of summer blossoms. "Thank you. I...thank you."

"When's my first appointment?"

"Nine-thirty. With Ms. Brinkman, Mr. Lowe and Mr. Keller, to finalize the buy on the housing project in New Jersey."

"That gives me about twenty minutes. I'd like to see you in my office."

"Yes, ma'am." Janine was already reaching for her pad.

"You won't need that," Sydney told her, and strode through the double doors. She seated herself, then gestured for Janine to take a chair.

"How long have you worked for Hayward?"

"Five years last March."

Sydney tipped back in her chair and looked at her secretary, really looked. Janine was attractive, neat, had direct gray eyes that were a trifle puzzled at the moment. Her dark blond hair was worn short and sleek. She held herself well, Sydney noted. Appearance was important, not the most important, but it certainly counted for what she was thinking.

"You must have been very young when you started here."

"Twenty-one," Janine answered with a small smile. "Right out of business college."

"Are you doing what you want to do, Janine?"

"Excuse me?"

"Is secretarial work what you want to do with your life, or do you have other ambitions?"

Janine resisted the urge to squirm in her chair. "I hope to work my way up to department manager. But I enjoy working for you, Miss Hayward."

"You have five years experience with the company, nearly five more than I do, yet you enjoy working for me. Why?"

"Why?" Janine stopped being nervous and went to flat-out baffled. "Being secretary to the president of Hayward is an important job, and I think I'm good at it."

"I agree with both statements." Rising, Sydney walked around the desk to perch on the front corner. "Let's be frank, Janine, no one here at Hayward expected me to stay more than a token month or two, and I'm sure it was generally agreed I'd spend most of that time filing my nails or chatting with friends on the phone." She saw by the faint flush that crept up Janine's cheeks that she'd hit very close to the mark. "They gave me an efficient secretary, not an assistant or an office manager, or executive aide, whatever we choose to call them at Hayward, because it wasn't thought I'd require one. True?"

"That's the office gossip." Janine straightened in her chair and met Sydney's eyes levelly. If she was about to be fired, she'd take it on the chin. "I took the job because it was a good position, a promotion and a raise."

"And I think you were very wise. The door opened, and you walked in. Since you've been working for me, you've been excellent. I can't claim to have a lot of experience in having a secretary, but I know that you're at your desk when I arrive in the morning and often stay after I leave at night. When I ask you for information you have it, or you get it. When I ask, you explain, and when I order, you get the job done.''

''I don't believe in doing things half way, Ms. Hayward.''

Sydney smiled, that was exactly what she wanted to hear. ''And you want to move up. Contrarily, when my position was tenuous at best last week, you stood behind me. Breaking into that board meeting was a risk, and putting yourself in my corner at that point certainly lessened your chances of moving up at Hayward had I been asked to step down. And it most certainly earned you a powerful enemy.''

''I work for you, not for Mr. Bingham. And even if it wasn't a matter of loyalty, you were doing what was right.''

''I feel very strongly about loyalty, Janine, just as strongly as I feel about giving someone who's trying to make something of herself the chance to do so. The flowers were a thank-you for that loyalty, from me to you, personally.''

''Thank you, Ms. Hayward.'' Janine's face relaxed in a smile.

''You're welcome. I consider your promotion to my executive assistant, with the appropriate salary and benefits, to be a good business decision.''

Janine's mouth dropped open. ''I beg your pardon?''

''I hope you'll accept the position, Janine. I need someone I trust, someone I respect, and someone who knows how the hell to run an office. Agreed?" Sydney offered a hand. Janine stared at it before she managed to rise and grip it firmly in hers.

"Ms. Hayward—"

"Sydney. We're going to be in this together."

Janine gave a quick, dazzled laugh. "Sydney. I hope I'm not dreaming."

"You're wide-awake, and the flak's going to fall before the day's over. Your first job in your new position is to arrange a meeting with Lloyd. Make it a formal request, here in my office before the close of business hours today."

He put her off until four-fifteen, but Sydney was patient. If anything, the extra time gave her the opportunity to examine her feelings and make certain her decision wasn't based on emotion.

When Janine buzzed him in, Sydney was ready, and she was sure.

"You picked a busy day for this," he began.

"Sit down, Lloyd."

He did, and she waited again while he took out a cigarette. "I won't take up much of your time," she told him. "I felt it best to discuss this matter as quickly as possible."

His gaze flicked up, and he smiled confidently through the haze of smoke. "Having problems on one of the projects?"

"No." Her lips curved in a wintry smile. "There's nothing I can't handle. It's the internal strife at Hayward that concerns me, and I've decided to remedy it."

"Office reorganization is a tricky business." He crossed his legs and leaned back. "Do you really think you've been around long enough to attempt it?"

"I'm not going to attempt it, I'm going to do it. I'd like your resignation on my desk by five o'clock tomorrow."

He bolted up. "What the hell are you talking about?"

"Your resignation, Lloyd. Or if necessary, your termination at Hayward. That distinction will be up to you."

He crushed the cigarette into pulp in the ashtray. "You think you can fire me? Walk in here with barely three months under your belt and fire me when I've been at Hayward for twelve years?"

"Here's the point," she said evenly. "Whether it's been three months or three days, I am Hayward. I will not tolerate one of my top executives undermining my position. It's obvious you're not happy with the current status at Hayward, and I can guarantee you, I'm going to remain in charge of this company for a long time. Therefore, I believe it's in your own interest, and certainly in mine, for you to resign."

"The hell I will."

"That's your choice, of course. I will, however, take the matter before the board, and use all the power at my disposal to limit yours."

Going with instinct, she pushed the next button. "Leaking Mrs. Wolburg's accident to the press didn't just put me in a difficult position. It put Hayward in a difficult position. As an executive vice president, your first duty is to the company, not to go off on some vindictive tangent because you dislike working for me.''

He stiffened, and she knew she'd guessed correctly. "You have no way of proving the leak came from my office.''

"You'd be surprised what I can prove," she bluffed. "I told you I wanted your loyalty or your resignation if the board stood behind me in the Soho project. We both know your loyalty is out of the question.''

"I'll tell you what you'll get." There was a sneer in his voice, but beneath the neat gray suit, he was sweating. "I'll be sitting behind that desk when you're back in Europe dancing from shop to shop.''

"No, Lloyd. You'll never sit behind this desk. As the major stockholder of Hayward, I'll see to that. Now," she continued quietly, "it wasn't necessary for me to document to the board the many cases in which you've ignored my requests, overlooked complaints from clients, tenants and other associates at the meeting on Friday. I will do so, however, at the next. In the current climate, I believe my wishes will be met.''

His fingers curled. He imagined the satisfaction of hooking them around her throat. "You think because you skidded through one mess, because your senile grandfather plopped you down at that desk, you can shoehorn me out? Lady, I'll bury you.''

Coolly she inclined her head. "You're welcome to try. If you don't manage it, it may be difficult for you to find a similar position with another company." Her eyes iced over. "If you don't think I have any influence, or the basic guts to carry this off, you're making a mistake. You have twenty-four hours to consider your options. This meeting is over.''

"Why you cold-blooded bitch."

She stood, and this time it was she who leaned over her desk. "Take me on," she said in a quiet voice. "Do it."

"This isn't over." Turning on his heel, he marched to the door to swing it open hard enough that it banged against the wall.

After three deep breaths, Sydney sank into her chair. Okay, she was shaking—but only a little. And it was temper, she realized as she pressed a testing hand against her stomach. Not fear. Good, solid temper. She found she didn't need to vent any anger by mangling paper clips or shredding stationery. In fact, she found she felt just wonderful.

Chapter Eight

Mikhail stirred the mixture of meats and spices and tomatoes in the old cast-iron skillet and watched the street below through his kitchen window. After a sniff and a taste, he added another splash of red wine to the mixture. Behind him in the living room *The Marriage of Figaro* soared from the stereo.

He wondered how soon Sydney would arrive.

Leaving the meal to simmer, he walked into the living room to study the rosewood block that was slowly becoming her face.

Her mouth. There was a softness about it that was just emerging. Testing, he measured it between his index finger and thumb. And remembered how it had tasted, moving eagerly under his. Hot candy, coated with cool, white wine. Addictive.

Those cheekbones, so aristocratic, so elegant. They could add a regal, haughty look one moment, or that of an ice-blooded warrior the next. That firm, proud jawline—he traced a fingertip along it and thought of how sensitive and smooth her skin was there.

Her eyes, he'd wondered if he'd have problems with her eyes. Oh, not the shape of them—that was basic to craft, but the feeling in them, the mysteries behind them.

There was still so much he needed to know.

He leaned closer until he was eye to eye with the half-formed bust. "You will let me in," he whispered. At the knock on the door, he stayed where he was, peering into Sydney's emerging face. "Is open."

"Hey, Mik." Keely breezed in wearing a polka-dotted T-shirt and shorts in neon green. "Got anything cold? My fridge finally gave up the ghost."

"Help yourself," he said absently, "I'll put you on top of the list for the new ones."

"My hero." She paused in the kitchen to sniff at the skillet. "God, this smells sinful." She tipped the spoon in and took a sample. "It is sinful. Looks like a lot for one."

"It's for two."

"Oh." She gave the word three ascending syllables as she pulled a soft drink out of the refrigerator. The smell was making her mouth water, and she glanced wistfully at the skillet again. "Looks like a lot for two, too."

He glanced over his shoulder and grinned. "Put some in a bowl. Simmer it a little longer."

"You're a prince, Mik." She rattled in his cupboards. "So who's the lucky lady?"

"Sydney Hayward."

"Sydney." Her eyes widened. The spoon she held halted in midair above the pan of bubbling goulash. "Hayward," she finished. "You mean the rich and beautiful Hayward who wears silk to work and carries a six-hundred-dollar purse, which I personally priced at Saks. She's coming here, to have dinner and everything?"

He was counting on the everything. "Yes."

"Gee." She couldn't think of anything more profound. But she wasn't sure she liked it. No, she wasn't sure at all, Keely thought as she scooped her impromptu dinner into a bowl.

The rich were different. She firmly believed it. And this lady was rich in capital letters. Keely knew Mikhail had earned some pretty big bucks with his art, but she couldn't think of him as rich. He was just Mik, the sexy guy next door who was always willing to unclog a sink or kill a spider or share a beer.

Carrying the bowl, she walked over to him and noticed his latest work in progress. "Oh," she said, but this time it was only a sigh. She would have killed for cheekbones like that.

"You like?"

"Sure, I always like your stuff." But she shifted from foot to foot. She didn't like the way he was looking at the face in the wood. "I, ah, guess you two have more than a business thing going."

"Yes." He hooked his thumbs in his pockets as he looked into Keely's troubled eyes. "This is a problem?"

"Problem? No, no problem." She worried her lower lip. "Well, it's just—boy, Mik, she's so uptown."

He knew she was talking about more than an address, but smiled and ran a hand over her hair. "You're worried for me."

"Well, we're pals, aren't we? I can't stand to see a pal get hurt."

Touched, he kissed her nose. "Like you did with the actor with the skinny legs?"

She moved her shoulders. "Yeah, I guess. But I wasn't in love with him or anything. Or only a little."

"You cried."

"Sure, but I'm a wienie. I tear up during greeting card commercials." Dissatisfied, she looked back at the bust. Definitely uptown. "A woman who looks like that, I figure she could drive a guy to joining the Foreign Legion or something."

He laughed and ruffled her hair. "Don't worry. I'll write."

Before she could think of anything else, there was another knock. Giving Keely a pat on the shoulder, he went to answer it.

"Hi." Sydney's face brightened the moment she saw him. She carried a garment bag in one hand and a bottle of champagne in the other. "Something smells wonderful. My mouth started watering on the third floor, and..." She spotted Keely standing near the worktable with a bowl cupped in her hands. "Hello." After clearing her throat, Sydney told herself she would not be embarrassed to have Mikhail's neighbor see her coming into his apartment with a suitcase.

"Hi. I was just going." Every bit as uncomfortable as Sydney, Keely darted back into the kitchen to grab her soft drink.

"It's nice to see you again." Sydney stood awkwardly beside the open door. "How did your murder go?"

"He strangled me in three takes." With a fleeting smile, she dashed through the door. "Enjoy your dinner. Thanks, Mik."

When the door down the hall slammed shut, Sydney let out a long breath. "Does she always move so fast?"

"Mostly." He circled Sydney's waist with his hands. "She is worried you will seduce me, use me, then toss me aside."

"Oh, well, really."

Chuckling, he nipped at her bottom lip. "I don't mind the first two." As his mouth settled more truly on hers, he slipped the garment bag out of her lax fingers and tossed it aside. Taking the bottle of wine, he used it to push the door closed at her back. "I like your dress. You look like a rose in sunshine."

Freed, her hands could roam along his back, slip under the chambray work shirt he hadn't tucked into his jeans. "I like the way you look, all the time."

His lips were curved as they pressed to her throat. "You're hungry?"

"Mmm. Past hungry. I had to skip lunch."

"Ten minutes," he promised, and reluctantly released her. If he didn't, dinner would be much, much later. "What have you brought us?" He twisted the bottle in his hand to study the label. One dark brow lifted. "This will humble my goulash."

With her eyes shut, Sydney took a long, appreciative sniff. "No, I don't think so." Then she laughed and took the bottle from him. "I wanted to celebrate. I had a really good day."

"You will tell me?"

"Yes."

"Good. Let's find some glasses that won't embarrass this champagne."

She didn't know when she'd been more charmed. He had set a small table and two chairs on the tiny balcony off the bedroom. A single pink peony graced an old green bottle in the center, and music drifted from his radio to lull the sounds of traffic. Thick blue bowls held the spicy stew, and rich black bread was heaped in a wicker basket.

While they ate, she told him about her decision to promote Janine, and her altercation with Lloyd.

"You ask for his resignation. You should fire him."

"It's a little more complicated than that." Flushed with success, Sydney lifted her glass to study the wine in the evening sunlight. "But the result's the same. If he pushes me, I'll have to go before the board. I have memos, other documentation. Take this building, for example." She tapped a finger on the old brick. "My grandfather turned it over to Lloyd more than a year ago with a request that he see to tenant demands and maintenance. You know the rest."

"Then perhaps I am grateful to him." He reached up to tuck her hair behind her ear, placing his lips just beneath the jet drops she wore. "If he had been honest and efficient, I wouldn't have had to be rude in your office. You might not be here with me tonight."

Taking his hand, she pressed it to her cheek. "Maybe I should have given him a raise." She turned her lips into his palm, amazed at how easy it had become for her to show her feelings.

"No. Instead, we'll think this was destiny. I don't like someone that close who would like to hurt you."

"I know he leaked Mrs. Wolburg's story to the press." Worked up again, Sydney broke off a hunk of bread. "His anger toward me caused him to put Hayward in a very unstable position. I won't tolerate that, and neither will the board."

"You'll fix it." He split the last of the champagne between them.

"Yes, I will." She was looking out over the neighborhood, seeing the clothes hung on lines to dry in the sun, the open windows where people could be seen walking by or sitting in front of televisions. There were children on the sidewalk taking advantage of a long summer day. When Mikhail's hand reached for hers, she gripped it tightly.

"Today, for the first time," she said quietly, "I felt in charge. My whole life I went along with what I was told was best or proper or expected." Catching herself, she shook her head. "That doesn't matter. What matters is that sometime over the last few months I started to realize that to be in charge meant you had to take charge. I finally did. I don't know if you can understand how that feels."

"I know what I see. And this is a woman who is beginning to trust herself, and take what is right for her." Smiling, he skimmed a finger down her cheek. "Take me."

She turned to him. He was less than an arm's length away. Those dark, untamed looks would have set any woman's heart leaping. But there was more happening to her than an excited pulse. She was afraid to consider it. There was only now, she reminded herself, and reached for him. He held her, rubbing his cheek against her hair, murmuring lovely words she couldn't understand.

"I'll have to get a phrase book." Her eyes closed on a sigh as his mouth roamed over her face.

"This one is easy." He repeated a phrase between kisses.

She laughed, moving willingly when he drew her to her feet. "Easy for you to say. What does it mean?"

His lips touched hers again. "I love you."

He watched her eyes fly open, saw the race of emotion in them run from shock to hope to panic. "Mikhail, I—"

"Why do the words frighten you?" he interrupted. "Love doesn't threaten."

"I didn't expect this." She put a hand to his chest to insure some distance. Eyes darkening, Mikhail looked down at it, then stepped back.

"What did you expect?"

"I thought you were…" Was there no delicate way? "I assumed that you…"

"Wanted only your body," he finished for her, and his voice heated. He had shown her so much, and she saw so little. "I do want it, but not only. Will you tell me there was nothing last night?"

"Of course not. It was beautiful." She had to sit down, really had to. It felt as though she'd jumped off a cliff and landed on her head. But he was looking at her in such a way that made her realize she'd better stay on her feet.

"The sex was good." He picked up his glass. Though he was tempted to fling it off the balcony, he only sipped. "Good sex is necessary for the body and for the state of mind. But it isn't enough for the heart. The heart needs love, and there was love last night. For both of us."

Her arms fell uselessly to her sides. "I don't know. I've never had good sex before."

He considered her over the rim of his glass. "You were not a virgin. You were married before."

"Yes, I was married before." And the taste of that was still bitter on her tongue. "I don't want to talk about that, Mikhail. Isn't it enough that we're good together, that I feel for you something I've never felt before? I don't want to analyze it. I just can't yet."

"You don't want to know what you feel?" That baffled him. "How can you live without knowing what's inside you?"

"It's different for me. I haven't had what you've had or done what you've done. And your emotions— they're always right there. You can see them in the way you move, the way you talk, in your eyes, in your work. Mine are...mine aren't as volatile. I need time."

He nearly smiled. "Do you think I'm a patient man?"

"No," she said, with feeling.

"Good. Then you'll understand that your time will be very short." He began to gather dishes. "Did this husband of yours hurt you?"

"A failed marriage hurts. Please, don't push me on that now."

"For tonight I won't." With the sky just beginning to deepen at his back, he looked at her. "Because tonight I want you only to think of me.'' He walked through the door, leaving her to gather the rest of the meal.

He loved her. The words swam in Sydney's mind as she picked up the basket and the flower. It wasn't possible to doubt it. She'd come to understand he was a man who said no more than he meant, and rarely less. But she couldn't know what love meant to him.

To her, it was something sweet and colorful and lasting that happened to other people. Her father had cared for her, in his erratic way. But they had only spent snatches of time together in her early childhood. After the divorce, when she'd been six, they had rarely seen each other.

And her mother. She didn't doubt her mother's affection. But she always realized it ran no deeper than any of Margerite's interests.

There had been Peter, and that had been strong and true and important. Until they had tried to love as husband and wife.

But it wasn't the love of a friend that Mikhail was offering her. Knowing it, feeling it, she was torn by twin forces of giddy happiness and utter terror.

With her mind still whirling, she walked into the kitchen to find him elbow deep in soapsuds. She set basket and bottle aside to pick up a dish towel.

''Are you angry with me?'' she ventured after a moment.

''Some. More I'm puzzled by you.'' And hurt, but he didn't want her guilt or pity. ''To be loved should make you happy, warm.''

''Part of me is. The other half is afraid of moving too fast and risking spoiling what we've begun.'' He needed honesty, she thought. Deserved it. She tried to give him what she had. "All day today I looked forward to being here with you, being able to talk to you, to be able to share with you what had happened. To listen to you. I knew you'd make me laugh, that my heart would speed up when you kissed me." She set a dry bowl aside. "Why are you looking at me like that?"

He only shook his head. "You don't even know you're in love with me. But it's all right," he decided, and offered her the next bowl. "You will."

"You're so arrogant," she said, only half-annoyed. "I'm never sure if I admire or detest that."

"You like it very much because it makes you want to fight back."

"I suppose you think I should be flattered because you love me."

"Of course." He grinned at her. "Are you?"

Thinking it over, she stacked the second bowl in the first, then took the skillet. "I suppose. It's human nature. And you're..."

"I'm what?"

She looked up at him again, the cocky grin, the dark amused eyes, the tumble of wild hair. "You're so gorgeous."

His grin vanished when his mouth dropped open. When he managed to close it again, he pulled his hands out of the water and began to mutter.

"Are you swearing at me?" Instead of answering her, he yanked the dishcloth away from her to dry his hands. "I think I embarrassed you." Delighted, she laughed and cupped his face in her hands. "Yes, I did."

"Stop." Thoroughly frazzled, he pushed her hands away. "I can't think of the word for what I am."

"But you are gorgeous." Before he could shake her off, she wound her arms around his neck. "When I first saw you, I thought you looked like a pirate, all dark and dashing."

This time he swore in English and she only smiled.

"Maybe it's the hair," she considered, combing her fingers through it. "I used to imagine what it would be like to get my hands in it. Or the eyes. So moody, so dangerous."

His hands lowered to her hips. "I'm beginning to feel dangerous."

"Hmm. Or the mouth. It just might be the mouth." She touched hers to it, then slowly, her eyes on his, outlined its shape with her tongue. "I can't imagine there's a woman still breathing who could resist it."

"You're trying to seduce me."

She let her hands slide down, her fingers toying with his buttons. "Somebody has to." She only hoped she could do it right. "Then, of course, there's this wonderful body. The first time I saw you without a shirt, I nearly swallowed my tongue." She parted his shirt to let her hands roam over his chest. His knees nearly buckled. "Your skin was wet and glistening, and there were all these muscles." She forgot the game, seducing herself as completely as him. "So hard, and the skin so smooth. I wanted to touch, like this."

Her breath shuddered out as she pressed her fingers into his shoulders, kneading her way down his arms. When her eyes focused on his again, she saw that they were fiercely intense. Beneath her fingers, his arms were taut as steel. The words dried up in her mouth.

"Do you know what you do to me?" he asked. He reached for the tiny black buttons on her jacket, and his fingers trembled. Beneath the sunny cap-sleeved suit, she wore lace the color of midnight. He could feel the fast dull thud of his heart in his head. "Or how much I need you?"

She could only shake her head. "Just show me. It's enough to show me."

She was caught fast and hard, her mouth fused to his, their bodies molded. When her arms locked around his neck, he lifted her an inch off the floor, circling slowly, his lips tangling with hers.

Dizzy and desperate, she clung to him as he wound his way into the bedroom. She kicked her shoes off, heedless of where they flew. There was such freedom in the simple gesture, she laughed, then held tight as they fell to the bed.

The mattress groaned and sagged, cupping them in the center. He was muttering her name, and she his, when their mouths met again.

It was as hot and reckless as before. Now she knew where they would go and strained to match his speed. The need to have him was as urgent as breath, and she struggled with his jeans, tugging at denim while he peeled away lace.

She could feel the nubs of the bedspread beneath her bare back, and him, hard and restless above her. Through the open window, the heat poured in. And there was a rumble, low and distant, of thunder. She felt the answering power echo in her blood.

He wanted the storm, outside, in her. Never before had he understood what it was to truly crave. He remembered hunger and a miserable wish for warmth. He remembered wanting the curves and softness of a woman. But all that was nothing, nothing like the violent need he felt for her.

His hands hurried over her, wanting to touch every inch, and everywhere he touched she burned. If she trembled, he drove her further until she shuddered. When she moaned, he took and tormented until she cried out.

And still he hungered.

Thunder stalked closer, like a threat. Following it through the window came the passionate wail of the sax. The sun plunged down in the sky, tossing flame and shadows.

Inside the hot, darkening room, they were aware of no time or sound. Reality had been whittled down to one man and one woman and the ruthless quest to mate.

He filled. She surrounded.

Crazed, he lifted her up until her legs circled his waist and her back arched like a bow. Shuddering from the power they made, he pressed his face to her shoulder and let it take him.

The rain held off until the next afternoon, then came with a full chorus of thunder and lightning. With her phone on speaker, Sydney handled a tricky conference call. Though Janine sat across from her, she took notes of her own. Thanks to a morning of intense work between herself and her new assistant, she had the information needed at her fingertips.

"Yes, Mr. Bernstein, I think the adjustments will be to everyone's benefit." She waited for the confirmation to run from Bernstein, to his lawyer, to his West Coast partner. "We'll have the revised draft faxed to all of you by five, East Coast time, tomorrow." She smiled to herself. "Yes, Hayward Industries believes in moving quickly. Thank you, gentlemen. Goodbye."

After disengaging the speaker, she glanced at Janine. "Well?"

"You never even broke a sweat. Look at me." Janine held out a hand. "My palms are wet. Those three were hoping to bulldoze you under and you came out dead even. Congratulations."

"I think that transaction should please the board." Seven million, she thought. She'd just completed a seven-million-dollar deal. And Janine was right. She was steady as a rock. "Let's get busy on the fine print, Janine."

"Yes, ma'am." Even as she rose, the phone rang. Moving on automatic, she plucked up Sydney's receiver. "Ms. Hayward's office. One moment, please." She clicked to hold. "Mr. Warfield."

The faintest wisp of fatigue clouded her eyes as she nodded. "I'll take it. Thank you, Janine."

She waited until her door closed again before bringing him back on the line. "Hello, Channing."

"Sydney, I've been trying to reach you for a couple of days. Where have you been hiding?"

She thought of Mikhail's lumpy bed and smiled. "I'm sorry, Channing. I've been...involved."

"All work and no play, darling," he said, and set her teeth on edge. "I'm going to take you away from all that. How about lunch tomorrow? Lutece."

As a matter of course, she checked her calendar. "I have a meeting."

"Meetings were made to be rescheduled."

"No, I really can't. As it is, I have a couple of projects coming to a head, and I won't be out of the office much all week."

"Now, Sydney, I promised Margerite I wouldn't let you bury yourself under the desk. I'm a man of my word."

Why was it, she thought, she could handle a multimillion-dollar deal with a cool head, but this personal pressure was making her shoulders tense? "My mother worries unnecessarily. I'm really sorry, Channing, but I can't chat now. I've got—I'm late for an appointment," she improvised.

"Beautiful women are entitled to be late. If I can't get you out to lunch, I have to insist that you come with us on Friday. We have a group going to the theater. Drinks first, of course, and a light supper after."

"I'm booked, Channing. Have a lovely time though. Now, I really must ring off. Ciao." Cursing herself, she settled the receiver on his pipe of protest.

Why hadn't she simply told him she was involved with someone?

Simple question, she thought, simple answer. Channing would go to Margerite, and Sydney didn't want her mother to know. What she had with Mikhail was hers, only hers, and she wanted to keep it that way for a little while longer.

He loved her.

Closing her eyes, she experienced the same quick trickle of pleasure and alarm. Maybe, in time, she would be able to love him back fully, totally, in the full-blooded way she was so afraid she was incapable of.

She'd thought she'd been frigid, too. She'd certainly been wrong there. But that was only one step.

Time, she thought again. She needed time to organize her emotions. And then . . . then they'd see.

The knock on her office door brought her back to earth. "Yes?"

"Sorry, Sydney." Janine came in carrying a sheet of Hayward stationery. "This just came in from Mr. Bingham's office. I thought you'd want to see it right away."

"Yes, thank you." Sydney scanned the letter. It was carefully worded to disguise the rage and bitterness, but it was a resignation. Effective immediately. Carefully she set the letter aside. It took only a marginal ability to read between the lines to know it wasn't over. "Janine, I'll need some personnel files. We'll want to fill Mr. Bingham's position, and I want to see if we can do it in-house."

"Yes, ma'am." She started toward the door, then stopped. "Sydney, does being your executive assistant mean I can offer advice?"

"It certainly does."

"Watch your back. There's a man who would love to stick a knife in it."

"I know. I don't intend to let him get behind me." She rubbed at the pressure at the back of her neck.

"Janine, before we deal with the files, how about some coffee? For both of us."

"Coming right up." She turned and nearly collided with Mikhail as he strode through the door. "Excuse me." The man was soaking wet and wore a plain white T-shirt that clung to every ridge of muscle. Janine entertained a brief fantasy of drying him off herself. "I'm sorry, Ms. Hayward is—"

"It's all right." Sydney was already coming around the desk. "I'll see Mr. Stanislaski."

Noting the look in her boss's eye, Janine managed to fight back the worst of the envy. "Shall I hold your calls?"

"Hmm?"

Mikhail grinned. "Please. You're Janine, with the promotion?"

"Why, yes."

"Sydney tells me you are excellent in your work."

"Thank you." Who would have thought the smell of wet male could be so terrific? "Would you like some coffee?"

"No, thank you."

"Hold mine, too, Janine. And take a break yourself."

"Yes, ma'am." With only a small envious sigh, she shut the door.

"Don't you have an umbrella?" Sydney asked him, and leaned forward for a kiss. He kept his hands to himself.

"I can't touch you, I'll mess up your suit. Do you have a towel?"

"Just a minute." She walked into the adjoining bath. "What are you doing uptown at this time of day?"

"The rain slows things up. I did paperwork and knocked off at four." He took the towel she offered and rubbed it over his head.

"Is it that late?" She glanced at the clock and saw it was nearly five.

"You're busy."

She thought of the resignation on her desk and the files she had to study. "A little."

"When you're not busy, maybe you'd like to go with me to the movies."

"I'd love to." She took the towel back. "I need an hour."

"I'll come back." He reached out to toy with the pearls at her throat. "There's something else."

"What?"

"My family goes to visit my sister this weekend. To have a barbecue. Will you go with me?"

"I'd love to go to a barbecue. When?"

"They leave Friday, after work." He wanted to sketch her in those pearls. Just those pearls. Though he rarely worked in anything but wood, he thought he might carve her in alabaster. "We can go when you're ready."

"I should be able to get home and changed by six. Six-thirty," she corrected. "All right?"

"All right." He took her shoulders, holding her a few inches away from his damp clothes as he kissed her. "Natasha will like you."

"I hope so."

He kissed her again. "I love you."

Emotion shuddered through her. "I know."

"And you love me," he murmured. "You're just stubborn." He toyed with her lips another moment. "But soon you'll pose for me."

"I...what?"

"Pose for me. I have a show in the fall, and I think I'll use several pieces of you."

"You never told me you had a show coming up." The rest of it hit her. "Of me?"

"Yes, we'll have to work very hard very soon. So now I leave you alone so you can work."

"Oh." She'd forgotten all about files and phone calls. "Yes, I'll see you in an hour."

"And this weekend there will be no work. But next..." He nodded, his mind made up. Definitely in alabaster.

She ran the damp towel through her hands as he walked to the door. "Mikhail."

With the door open, he stood with his hand on the knob. "Yes?"

"Where does your sister live?"

"West Virginia." He grinned and shut the door behind her. Sydney stared at the blank panel for a full ten seconds.

"West Virginia?"

Chapter Nine

She'd never be ready in time. Always decisive about her wardrobe, Sydney had packed and unpacked twice. What did one wear for a weekend in West Virginia? A few days in Martinique—no problem. A quick trip to Rome would have been easy. But a weekend, a family weekend in West Virginia, had her searching frantically through her closet.

As she fastened her suitcase a third time, she promised herself she wouldn't open it again. To help herself resist temptation, she carried the bag into the living room, then hurried back to the bedroom to change out of her business suit.

She'd just pulled on thin cotton slacks and a sleeveless top in mint green—and was preparing to tear them off again—when the knock sounded at her door.

It would have to do. It would do, she assured herself as she went to answer. They would be arriving so late at his sister's home, it hardly mattered what she was wearing. With a restless hand she brushed her hair back, wondered if she should secure it with a scarf for the drive, then opened the door.

Sequined and sleek, Margerite stood on the other side.

"Sydney, darling." As she glided inside, she kissed her daughter's cheek.

"Mother. I didn't know you were coming into the city today."

"Of course you did." She settled into a chair, crossed her legs. "Channing told you about our little theater party."

"Yes, he did. I'd forgotten."

"Sydney." The name was a sigh. "You're making me worry about you."

Automatically Sydney crossed to the liquor cabinet to pour Margerite a glass of her favored brand of sherry. "There's no need. I'm fine."

"No need?" Margerite's pretty coral-tipped fingers fluttered. "You turn down dozens of invitations, couldn't even spare an afternoon to shop with your mother last week, bury yourself in that office for positively hours on end. And there's no need for me to worry." She smiled indulgently and she accepted the glass. "Well, we're going to fix all of that. I want you to go in and change into something dashing. We'll meet Channing and the rest of the party at Doubles for a drink before curtain."

The odd thing was, Sydney realized, she'd very nearly murmured an agreement, so ingrained was her habit of doing what was expected of her. Instead, she perched on the arm of the sofa and hoped she could do this without hurting Margerite's feelings.

"Mother, I'm sorry. If I've been turning down invitations, it's because the transition at Hayward is taking up most of my time and energy."

"Darling." Margerite gestured with the glass before she sipped. "That's exactly my point."

But Sydney only shook her head. "And the simple fact is, I don't feel the need to have my social calendar filled every night any longer. As for tonight, I appreciate, I really do, the fact that you'd like me to join you. But, as I explained to Channing, I have plans."

Irritation sparked in Margerite's eyes, but she only tapped a nail on the arm of the chair. "If you think I'm going to leave you here to spend the evening cooped up with some sort of nasty paperwork—"

"I'm not working this weekend," Sydney interrupted. "Actually, I'm going out of town for—" The quick rap at the door relieved her. "Excuse me a minute." The moment she'd opened the door, Sydney reached out a hand for him. "Mikhail, my—"

Obviously he didn't want to talk until he'd kissed her, which he did, thoroughly, in the open doorway. Pale and rigid, Margerite pushed herself to her feet. She understood, as a woman would, that the kiss she was witnessing was the kind exchanged by lovers.

"Mikhail." Sydney managed to draw back an inch. "I'm not finished yet."

One hand braced against his chest as she gestured helplessly with the other. "My mother..."

He glanced over, caught the white-faced fury and shifted Sydney easily to his side. A subtle gesture of protection. "Margerite."

"Isn't there a rule," she said stiffly, "about mixing business and pleasure?" She lifted her brows as her gaze skimmed over him. "But then, you wouldn't be a rule follower, would you, Mikhail?"

"Some rules are important, some are not." His voice was gentle, but without regret and without apology. "Honesty is important, Margerite. I was honest with you."

She turned away, refusing to acknowledge the truth of that. "I'd prefer a moment with you, alone, Sydney."

There was a pounding at the base of her skull as she looked at her mother's rigid back. "Mikhail, would you take my bag to the car? I'll be down in a few minutes."

He cupped her chin, troubled by what he read in her eyes. "I'll stay with you."

"No." She put a hand to his wrist. "It would be best if you left us alone. Just a few minutes." Her fingers tightened. "Please."

She left him no choice. Muttering to himself, he picked up her suitcase. The moment the door closed behind him, Margerite whirled. Sydney was already braced. It was rare, very rare for Margerite to go on a tirade. But when she did, it was always an ugly scene with vicious words.

"You fool. You've been sleeping with him."

"I don't see that as your concern. But, yes, I have."

"Do you think you have the sense or skill to handle a man like that?" There was the crack of glass against wood as she slapped the little crystal goblet onto the table. "This sordid little liaison could ruin you, ruin everything I've worked for. God knows you did enough damage by divorcing Peter, but I managed to put that right. Now this. Sneaking off for a weekend at some motel."

Sydney's fists balled at her sides. "There is nothing sordid about my relationship with Mikhail, and I'm not sneaking anywhere. As for Peter, I will not discuss him with you."

Eyes hard, Margerite stepped forward. "From the day you were born, I used everything at my disposal to be certain you had what you deserved as a Hayward. The finest schools, the proper friends, even the right husband. Now, you're tossing it all back at me, all the planning, all the sacrificing. And for what?"

She whirled around the room as Sydney remained stiff and silent.

"Oh, believe me, I understand that man's appeal. I'd even toyed with the idea of having a discreet affair with him myself." The wound to her vanity was raw and throbbing. "A woman's entitled to a wild fling with a magnificent animal now and again. And his artistic talents and reputation are certainly in his favor. But his background is nothing, less than nothing. Gypsies and farmers and peasants. I have the experience to handle him—had I chosen to. I also have no ties at the moment to make an affair awkward. You, however, are on the verge of making a commitment to Channing. Do you think he'd have you if he ever learned you'd been taking that magnificent brute to bed?"

"That's enough." Sydney moved forward to take her mother's arm. "That's past enough. For someone who's so proud of the Hayward lineage, you certainly made no attempt to keep the name yourself. It was always my burden to be a proper Hayward, to do nothing to damage the Hayward name. Well, I've been a proper Hayward, and right now I'm working day and night to be certain the Hayward name remains above reproach. But my personal time, and whom I decide to spend that personal time with, is my business."

Pale with shock, Margerite jerked her hand away. Not once, from the day she'd been born, had Sydney spoken to her in such a manner. "Don't you dare use that tone with me. Are you so blinded with lust that you've forgotten where your loyalties lie?"

"I've never forgotten my loyalties," Sydney tossed back. "And at the moment, this is the most reasonable tone I can summon." It surprised her as well, this fast, torrid venom, but she couldn't stop it. "Listen to me, Mother, as far as Channing goes, I have never been on the verge of making a commitment to him, nor do I ever intend to do so. That's what you intended. And I will never, never, be pressured into making that kind of commitment again. If it would help disabuse Channing of the notion, I'd gladly take out a full-page ad in the *Times* announcing my relationship with Mikhail. As to that, you know nothing about Mikhail's family, you know nothing about him, as a man. You never got beyond his looks."

Margerite's chin lifted. "And you have?"

"Yes, I have, and he's a caring, compassionate man. An honest man who knows what he wants out of life and goes after it. You'd understand that, but the difference is he'd never use or hurt anyone to get it. He loves me. And I..." It flashed through her like light, clear, warm and utterly simple. "I love him."

"Love?" Stunned, Margerite reared back. "Now I know you've taken leave of your senses. My God, Sydney, do you believe everything a man says in bed?"

"I believe what Mikhail says. Now, I'm keeping him waiting, and we have a long trip to make."

Head high, chin set, Margerite streamed toward the door, then tossed a last look over her shoulder. "He'll break your heart, and make a fool of you in the bargain. But perhaps that's what you need to remind you of your responsibilities."

When the door snapped shut, Sydney lowered onto the arm of the sofa. Mikhail would have to wait another moment.

He wasn't waiting; he was prowling. Back and forth in front of the garage elevators he paced, hands jammed into his pockets, thoughts as black as smoke. When the elevator doors slid open, he was on Sydney in a heartbeat.

"Are you all right?" He had her face in his hands. "No, I can see you are not."

"I am, really. It was unpleasant. Family arguments always are."

For him, family arguments were fierce and furious and inventive. They could either leave him enraged or laughing, but never drained as she was now. "Come, we can go upstairs, leave in the morning when you're feeling better."

"No, I'd like to go now."

"I'm sorry." He kissed both of her hands. "I don't like to cause bad feelings between you and your mama."

"It wasn't you. Really." Because she needed it, she rested her head on his chest, soothed when his arms came around her. "It was old business, Mikhail, buried too long. I don't want to talk about it."

"You keep too much from me, Sydney."

"I know. I'm sorry." She closed her eyes, feeling her stomach muscles dance, her throat drying up. It couldn't be so hard to say the words. "I love you, Mikhail."

The hand stroking her back went still, then dived into her hair to draw her head back. His eyes were intense, like two dark suns searching hers. He saw what he wanted to see, what he needed desperately to see. "So, you've stopped being stubborn." His voice was thick with emotion, and his mouth, when it met hers, gave her more than dozens of soft endearments. "You can tell me again while we drive. I like to hear it."

Laughing, she linked an arm through his as they walked to the car. "All right."

"And while you drive, I tell you."

Eyes wide, she stopped. "I drive?"

"Yes." He opened the passenger door for her. "I start, then you have a turn. You have license, yes?"

She glanced dubiously at the gauges on the dash. "Yes."

"You aren't afraid?"

She looked back up to see him grinning. "Not tonight, I'm not."

* * *

It was after midnight when Mikhail pulled up at the big brick house in Shepherdstown. It was cooler now. There wasn't a cloud in the star-scattered sky to hold in the heat. Beside him, Sydney slept with her head resting on a curled fist. He remembered that she had taken the wheel on the turnpike, driving from New Jersey into Delaware with verve and enthusiasm. Soon after they'd crossed the border into Maryland and she'd snuggled into the passenger seat again, she'd drifted off.

Always he had known he would love like this. That he would find the one woman who would change the zigzagging course of his life into a smooth circle. She was with him now, dreaming in an open car on a quiet road.

When he looked at her, he could envision how their lives would be. Not perfectly. To see perfectly meant there would be no surprises. But he could imagine waking beside her in the morning, in the big bedroom of the old house they would buy and make into a home together. He could see her coming home at night, wearing one of those pretty suits, her face reflecting the annoyance or the success of the day. And they would sit together and talk, of her work, of his.

One day, her body would grow ripe with child. He would feel their son or daughter move inside her. And they would fill their home with children and watch them grow.

But he was moving too quickly. They had come far already, and he wanted to treasure each moment.

He leaned over to nuzzle his lips over her throat. "I've crossed the states with you, *milaya*." She stirred, murmuring sleepily. "Over rivers and mountains. Kiss me."

She came awake with his mouth warm on hers and her hand resting against his cheek. She felt the flutter of a night breeze on her skin and smelled the fragrance of roses and honeysuckle. And the stir of desire was just as warm, just as sweet.

"Where are we?"

"The sign said, Wild, Wonderful West Virginia." He nipped at her lip. "You will tell me if you think it is so."

Any place, any place at all was wild and wonderful, when he was there, she thought as her arms came around him. He gave a quiet groan, then a grunt as the gearshift pressed into a particularly sensitive portion of his anatomy. "I must be getting old. It is not so easy as it was to seduce a woman in a car."

"I thought you were doing a pretty good job."

He felt the quick excitement stir his blood, fantasized briefly, then shook his head. "I'm intimidated because my mama may peek out the window any minute. Come. We'll find your bed, then I'll sneak into it."

She laughed as he unfolded his long legs out of the open door. "Now I'm intimidated." Pushing her hair back, she turned to look at the house. It was big and brick, with lights glowing gold in the windows of the first floor. Huge leafy trees shaded it, pretty box hedges shielded it from the street.

When Mikhail joined her with their bags, they started up the stone steps that cut through the slope of lawn. And here were the flowers, the roses she had smelled, and dozens of others. No formal garden this, but a splashy display that seemed to grow wild and willfully. She saw the shadow of a tricycle near the porch. In the spill of light from the windows, she noted that a bed of petunias had been recently and ruthlessly dug up.

"I think Ivan has been to work," Mikhail commented, noting the direction of Sydney's gaze. "If he is smart, he hides until it's time to go home again."

Before they had crossed the porch, she heard the laughter and music.

"It sounds as though they're up," Sydney said. "I thought they might have gone to bed."

"We have only two days together. We won't spend much of it sleeping." He opened the screen door and entered without knocking. After setting the bags near the stairs, then taking Sydney's hand, he dragged her down the hall toward the party sounds.

Sydney could feel her reserve settling back into place. She couldn't help it. All the early training, all the years of schooling had drummed into her the proper way to greet strangers. Politely, coolly, giving no more of yourself than a firm handshake and a quiet "how do you do."

She'd hardly made the adjustment when Mikhail burst into the music room, tugging her with him.

"Ha," he said, and swooped down on a small, gorgeous woman in a purple sundress. She laughed when he scooped her up, her black mane of curling hair flying out as he swung her in a circle.

"You're always late," Natasha said. She kissed her brother on both cheeks then the lips. "What did you bring me?"

"Maybe I have something in my bag for you." He set her on her feet, then turned to the man at the piano. "You take good care of her?"

"When she lets me." Spence Kimball rose to clasp hands with Mikhail. "She's been fretting for you for an hour."

"I don't fret," Natasha corrected, turning to Sydney. She smiled—the warmth was automatic—though what she saw concerned her. This cool, distant woman was the one her family insisted Mikhail was in love with? "You haven't introduced me to your friend."

"Sydney Hayward." A little impatient by the way Sydney hung back, he nudged her forward. "My sister, Natasha."

"It's nice to meet you." Sydney offered a hand. "I'm sorry about being so late. It's really my fault."

"I was only teasing. You're welcome here. You already know my family." They were gathering around Mikhail as if it had been years since the last meeting. "And this is my husband, Spence."

But he was stepping forward, puzzlement and pleasure in his eyes. "Sydney? Sydney Hayward?"

She turned, the practiced smile in place. It turned to surprise and genuine delight. "Spence Kimball. I had no idea." Offering both hands, she gripped his. "Mother told me you'd moved south and remarried."

"You've met," Natasha observed, exchanging looks with her own mother as Nadia brought over fresh glasses of wine.

"I've known Sydney since she was Freddie's age," Spence answered, referring to his eldest daughter. "I haven't seen her since..." He trailed off, remembering the last time had been at her wedding. Spence may have been out of touch with New York society in recent years, but he was well aware the marriage hadn't worked out.

"It's been a long time," Sydney murmured, understanding perfectly.

"Is small world," Yuri put in, slapping Spence on the back with fierce affection. "Sydney is owner of building where Mikhail lives. Until she pays attention to him, he sulks."

"I don't sulk." Grumbling a bit, Mikhail took his father's glass and tossed back the remaining vodka in it. "I convince. Now she is crazy for me."

"Back up, everyone," Rachel put in, "his ego's expanding again."

Mikhail merely reached over and twisted his sister's nose. "Tell them you're crazy for me," he ordered Sydney, "so this one eats her words."

Sydney lifted a brow. "How do you manage to speak when your mouth's so full of arrogance?"

Alex hooted and sprawled onto the couch. "She has your number, Mikhail. Come over here, Sydney, and sit beside me. I'm humble."

"You tease her enough for tonight." Nadia shot Alex a daunting look. "You are tired after your drive?" she asked Sydney.

"A little. I—"

"I'm sorry." Instantly Natasha was at her side. "Of course you're tired. I'll show you your room." She was already leading Sydney out. "If you like you can rest, or come back down. We want you to be at home while you're here."

"Thank you," Sydney replied. Before she could reach for her bag, Natasha had hefted it. "It's kind of you to have me."

Natasha merely glanced over her shoulder. "You're my brother's friend, so you're mine." But she certainly intended to grill Spence before the night was over.

At the end of the hall, she took Sydney into a small room with a narrow four-poster. Faded rugs were tossed over a gleaming oak floor. Snapdragons spiked out of an old milk bottle on a table by the window where gauzy Priscillas fluttered in the breeze.

"I hope you're comfortable here." Natasha set the suitcase on a cherrywood trunk at the foot of the bed.

"It's charming." The room smelled of the cedar wardrobe against the wall and the rose petals scattered in a bowl on the nightstand. "I'm very happy to meet Mikhail's sister, and the wife of an old friend. I'd heard Spence was teaching music at a university."

"He teaches at Shepherd College. And he composes again."

"That's wonderful. He's tremendously talented." Feeling awkward, she traced a finger over the wedding ring quilt. "I remember his little girl, Freddie."

"She is ten now." Natasha's smile warmed. "She tried to wait up for Mikhail, but fell asleep on the couch." Her chin angled. "She took Ivan with her to bed, thinking I would not strangle him there. He dug up my petunias. Tomorrow, I think . . ."

She trailed off, head cocked.

"Is something wrong?"

"No, it's Katie, our baby." Automatically Natasha laid a hand on her breast where her milk waited. "She wakes for a midnight snack. If you'll excuse me."

"Of course."

At the door, Natasha hesitated. She could go with her instincts or her observations. She'd always trusted her instincts. "Would you like to see her?"

After only an instant's hesitation, Sydney's lips curved. "Yes, very much."

Across the hall and three doors down, the sound of the child's restless crying was louder. The room was softly lit by a nightlight in the shape of a pink sea horse.

"There, sweetheart." Natasha murmured in two languages as she lifted her baby from the crib. "Mama's here now." As the crying turned to a soft whimpering, Natasha turned to see Spence at the doorway. "I have her. She's wet and hungry, that's all."

But he had to come in. He never tired of looking at his youngest child, that perfect and beautiful replica of the woman he'd fallen in love with. Bending close, his cheek brushing his wife's, he stroked a finger over Katie's. The whimpering stopped completely, and the gurgling began.

"You're just showing off for Sydney," Natasha said with a laugh.

While Sydney watched, they cuddled the baby. There was a look exchanged over the small dark head, a look of such intimacy and love and power that it brought tears burning in her throat. Unbearably moved, she slipped out silently and left them alone.

She was awakened shortly past seven by high, excited barking, maniacal laughter and giggling shouts coming from outside her window. Moaning a bit, she turned over and found the bed empty.

Mikhail had lived up to his promise to sneak into her room, and she doubted either of them found sleep in the narrow bed much before dawn.

But he was gone now.

Rolling over, she put the pillow over her head to smother the sounds from the yard below. Since it also smothered her, she gave it up. Resigned, she climbed out of bed and pulled on her robe. She just managed to find the doorknob and open the door, when Rachel opened the one across the hall.

The two disheveled women gave each other bleary-eyed stares. Rachel yawned first.

"When I have kids," she began, "they're not going to be allowed out of bed until ten on Saturday mornings. Noon on Sunday. And only if they're bringing me breakfast in bed."

Sydney ran her tongue over her teeth, propping herself on the doorjamb. "Good luck."

"I wish I wasn't such a sucker for them." She yawned again. "Got a quarter?"

Because she was still half-asleep, Sydney automatically searched the pockets of her robe. "No, I'm sorry."

"Hold on." Rachel disappeared into her room, then came back out with a coin. "Call it."

"Excuse me?"

"Heads or tails. Winner gets the shower first. Loser has to go down and get the coffee."

"Oh." Her first inclination was to be polite and offer to get the coffee, then she thought of a nice hot shower. "Tails."

Rachel flipped, caught the coin and held it out. "Damn. Cream and sugar?"

"Black."

"Ten minutes," Rachel promised, then started down the hall. She stopped, glanced around to make sure they were alone. "Since it's just you and me, are you really crazy about Mikhail?"

"Since it's just you and me, yes."

Rachel's grin was quick and she rocked back on her heels. "I guess there's no accounting for taste."

Thirty minutes later, refreshed by the shower and coffee, Sydney wandered downstairs. Following the sounds of activity, she found most of the family had centered in the kitchen for the morning.

Natasha stood at the stove in a pair of shorts and a T-shirt. Yuri sat at the table, shoveling in pancakes and making faces at the giggling baby who was strapped into one of those clever swings that rocked and played music. Alex slouched with his head in his hands, barely murmuring when his mother shoved a mug of coffee under his nose.

"Ah, Sydney."

Alex winced at his father's booming greeting. "Papa, have some respect for the dying."

He only gave Alex an affectionate punch on the arm. "You come sit beside me," Yuri instructed Sydney. "And try Tash's pancakes."

"Good morning," Natasha said even as her mother refilled Sydney's coffee cup. "I apologize for my barbaric children and the mongrel who woke the entire house so early."

"Children make noise," Yuri said indulgently. Katie expressed agreement by squealing and slamming a rattle onto the tray of the swing.

"Everyone's up then?" Sydney took her seat.

"Spence is showing Mikhail the barbecue pit he built," Natasha told her and set a heaping platter of pancakes on the table. "They'll stand and study and make men noises. You were comfortable in the night?"

Sydney thought of Mikhail and struggled not to blush. "Yes, thank you. Oh, please," she started to protest when Yuri piled pancakes on her plate.

"For energy," he said, and winked.

Before she could think how to respond, a small curly-haired bullet shot through the back door. Yuri caught him on the fly and hauled the wriggling bundle into his arms.

"This is my grandson, Brandon. He is monster. And I eat monsters for breakfast. Chomp, chomp."

The boy of about three was wiry and tough, squirming and squealing on Yuri's lap. "Papa, come watch me ride my bike. Come watch me!"

"You have a guest," Nadia said mildly, "and no manners."

Resting his head against Yuri's chest, Brandon gave Sydney a long, owlish stare. "You can come watch me, too," he invited. "You have pretty hair. Like Lucy."

"That's a very high compliment," Natasha told her. "Lucy is a cat. Miss Hayward can watch you later. She hasn't finished her breakfast."

"You watch, Mama."

Unable to resist, Natasha rubbed a hand over her son's curls. "Soon. Go tell your daddy he has to go to the store for me."

"Papa has to come."

Knowing the game, Yuri huffed and puffed and stuck Brandon on his shoulders. The boy gave a shout of laughter and gripped tight to Yuri's hair as his grandfather rose to his feet.

"Daddy, look! Look how tall I am," Brandon was shouting as they slammed out of the screen door.

"Does the kid ever stop yelling?" Alex wanted to know.

"You didn't stop yelling until you were twelve," Nadia told him, and added a flick with her dishcloth.

Feeling a little sorry for him, Sydney rose to pour more coffee into his mug herself. He snatched her hand and brought it to his lips for a smacking kiss. "You're a queen among women, Sydney. Run away with me."

"Do I have to kill you?" Mikhail asked as he strolled into the kitchen.

Alex only grinned. "We can arm wrestle for her."

"God, men are such pigs," Rachel observed as she walked in from the opposite direction.

"Why?" The question came from a pretty, golden-haired girl who popped through the doorway, behind Mikhail.

"Because, Freddie, they think they can solve everything with muscles and sweat instead of their tiny little brains."

Ignoring his sister, Mikhail pushed plates aside, sat down and braced an elbow on the table. Alex grinned at the muttered Ukrainian challenge. Palms slapped together.

"What are they doing?" Freddie wanted to know.

"Being silly." Natasha sighed and swung an arm around Freddie's shoulder. "Sydney, this is my oldest, Freddie. Freddie, this is Miss Hayward, Mikhail's friend."

Disconcerted, Sydney smiled at Freddie over Mikhail's head. "It's nice to see you again, Freddie. I met you a long time ago when you were just a baby."

"Really?" Intrigued, Freddie was torn between studying Sydney or watching Mikhail and Alex. They were knee to knee, hands clasped, and the muscles in their arms were bulging.

"Yes, I, ah..." Sydney was having a problem herself. Mikhail's eyes flicked up and over her before returning to his brother's. "I knew your father when you lived in New York."

There were a couple of grunts from the men at the table. Rachel sat at the other end and helped herself to pancakes. "Pass me the syrup."

With his free hand, Mikhail shoved it at her.

Smothering a grin, Rachel poured lavishly. "Mama, do you want to take a walk into town after I eat?"

"That would be nice." Ignoring her sons, Nadia began to load the dishwasher. She preferred the arm wrestling to the rolling and kicking they'd treated each other to as boys. "We can take Katie in the stroller if you like, Natasha."

"I'll walk in with you, and check on the shop." Natasha washed her hands. "I own a toy store in town," she told Sydney.

"Oh." Sydney couldn't take her eyes off the two men. Natasha could very well have told her she owned a missile site. "That's nice."

The three Stanislaski women grinned at each other. Sentimental, Nadia began to imagine a fall wedding. "Would you like more coffee?" she asked Sydney.

"Oh, I—"

Mikhail gave a grunt of triumph as he slapped his brother's arm on the table. Dishes jumped. Caught up in the moment, Freddie clapped and had her baby sister mimicking the gesture.

Grinning, Alex flexed his numbed fingers. "Two out of three."

"Get your own woman." Before Sydney could react, Mikhail scooped her up, planted a hard kiss on her mouth that tasted faintly and erotically of sweat, then carried her out the door.

Chapter Ten

"**Y**ou might have lost, you know."

Amused by the lingering annoyance in her voice, Mikhail slid an arm around Sydney's waist and continued to walk down the sloping sidewalk. "I didn't."

"The point—" She sucked in her breath. She'd been trying to get the point through that thick Slavic skull off and on for more than an hour. "The point is that you and Alex arm wrestled for me as if I were a six-pack of beer."

His grin only widened, a six-pack would make him a little drunk, but that was nothing to what he'd felt when he'd looked up and seen the fascination in her eyes as she'd stared at his biceps. He flexed them a little, believing a man had a right to vanity.

"And then," she continued, making sure her voice was low, as his family was wandering along in front and behind them. "You manhandled me—in front of your mother."

"You liked it."

"I certainly—"

"Did," he finished, remembering the hot, helpless way she'd responded to the kiss he'd given her on his sister's back porch. "So did I."

She would not smile. She would not admit for a moment to the spinning excitement she'd felt when he'd scooped her up like some sweaty barbarian carrying off the spoils of war.

"Maybe I was rooting for Alex. It seems to me he got the lion's share of your father's charm."

"All the Stanislaskis have charm," he said, unoffended. He stopped and, bending down, plucked a painted daisy from the slope of the lawn they passed. "See?"

"Hmm." Sydney twirled the flower under her nose. Perhaps it was time to change the subject before she was tempted to try to carry him off. "It's good seeing Spence again. When I was fifteen or so, I had a terrible crush on him."

Narrow eyed, Mikhail studied his brother-in-law's back. "Yes?"

"Yes. Your sister's a lucky woman."

Family pride came first. "He's lucky to have her."

This time she did smile. "I think we're both right."

Brandon, tired of holding his mother's hand, bolted back toward them. "You have to carry me," he told his uncle.

"Have to?"

With an enthusiastic nod, Brandon began to shimmy up Mikhail's leg like a monkey up a tree. "Like Papa does."

Mikhail hauled him up, then to the boy's delight, carried him for a while upside down.

"He'll lose his breakfast," Nadia called out.

"Then we fill him up again." But Mikhail flipped him over so Brandon could cling to his back. Pink cheeked, the boy grinned over at Sydney.

"I'm three years old," he told her loftily. "And I can dress my own self."

"And very well, too." Amused, she tapped his sneakered foot. "Are you going to be a famous composer like your father?"

"Nah. I'm going to be a water tower. They're the biggest."

"I see." It was the first time she'd heard quite so grand an ambition.

"Do you live with Uncle Mikhail?"

"No," she said quickly.

"Not yet," Mikhail said simultaneously, and grinned at her.

"You were kissing him," Brandon pointed out. "How come you don't have any kids?"

"That's enough questions." Natasha came to the rescue, plucking her son from Mikhail's back as her brother roared with laughter.

"I just wanna know—"

"Everything," Natasha supplied, and gave him a smacking kiss. "But for now it's enough you know you can have one new car from the shop."

He forgot all about babies. His chocolate-brown eyes turned shrewd. "Any car?"

"Any *little* car."

"You did kiss me," Mikhail reminded Sydney as Brandon began to badger his mother about how little was little. Sydney settled the discussion by ramming her elbow into Mikhail's ribs.

She found the town charming, with its sloping streets and little shops. Natasha's toy store, The Fun House, was impressive, its stock running the range from tiny plastic cars to exquisite porcelain dolls and music boxes.

Mikhail proved to be cooperative when Sydney wandered in and out of antique shops, craft stores and boutiques. Somewhere along the line they'd lost the rest of the family. Or the family had lost them. It wasn't until they'd started back, uphill, with his arms loaded with purchases that he began to complain.

"Why did I think you were a sensible woman?"

"Because I am."

He muttered one of the few Ukrainian phrases she understood. "If you're so sensible, why did you buy all this? How do you expect to get it back to New York?"

Pleased with herself, she fiddled with the new earrings she wore. The pretty enameled stars swung jauntily. "You're so clever, I knew you'd find a way."

"Now you're trying to flatter me, and make me stupid."

She smiled. "You were the one who bought me the porcelain box."

Trapped, he shook his head. She'd studied the oval box, its top decorated with a woman's serene face in bas-relief for ten minutes, obviously in love and just

as obviously wondering if she should be extravagant.
"You were mooning over it."

"I know." She rose on her toes to kiss his cheek.
"Thank you."

"You won't thank me when you have to ride for five
hours with all this on your lap."

They climbed to the top of the steps into the yard
just as Ivan, tail tucked securely between his legs
streaked across the grass. In hot pursuit were a pair of
long, lean cats. Mikhail let out a manful sigh.

"He is an embarrassment to the family."

"Poor little thing." Sydney shoved the package she
carried at Mikhail. "Ivan!" She clapped her hands
and crouched down. "Here, boy."

Spotting salvation, he swung about, scrambled for
footing and shot back in her direction. Sydney caught
him up, and he buried his trembling head against her
neck. The cats, sinuous and smug, sat down a few feet
away and began to wash.

"Hiding behind a woman," Mikhail said in disgust.

"He's just a baby. Go arm wrestle with your
brother."

Chuckling, he left her to soothe the traumatized
pup. A moment later, panting, Freddie rounded the
side of the house. "There he is."

"The cats frightened him," Sydney explained, as
Freddie came up to stroke Ivan's fur.

"They were just playing. Do you like puppies?"
Freddie asked.

"Yes." Unable to resist, Sydney nuzzled. "Yes, I
do."

"Me, too. And cats. We've had Lucy and Desi for a long time. Now I'm trying to talk Mama into a puppy." Petting Ivan, she looked back at the mangled petunias. "I thought maybe if I fixed the flowers."

Sydney knew what it was to be a little girl yearning for a pet. "It's a good start. Want some help?"

She spent the next thirty minutes saving what flowers she could or—since she'd never done any gardening—following Freddie's instructions. The pup stayed nearby, shivering when the cats strolled up to wind around legs or be scratched between the ears.

When the job was done, Sydney left Ivan to Freddie's care and went inside to wash up. It occurred to her that it was barely noon and she'd done several things that day for the first time.

She'd been the grand prize in an arm wrestling contest. She'd played with children, been kissed by the man she loved on a public street. She'd gardened and had sat on a sunny lawn with a puppy on her lap.

If the weekend kept going this way, there was no telling what she might experience next.

Attracted by shouts and laughter, she slipped into the music room and looked out the window. A softball game, she realized. Rachel was pitching, one long leg cocking back as she whizzed one by Alex. Obviously displeased by the call, he turned to argue with his mother. She continued to shake her head at him, bouncing Brandon on her knee as she held firm to her authority as umpire.

Mikhail stood spread legged, his hands on his hips, and one heel touching a ripped seat cushion that stood in as second base. He tossed in his own opinion, and

Rachel threw him a withering glance over her shoulder, still displeased that he'd caught a piece of her curve ball.

Yuri and Spence stood in the outfield, catcalling as Alex fanned for a second strike. Intrigued, Sydney leaned on the windowsill. How beautiful they were, she thought. She watched as Brandon turned to give Nadia what looked like a very sloppy kiss before he bounded off on sturdy little legs toward a blue-and-white swing set. A screen door slammed, then Freddie zoomed into view, detouring to the swing to give her brother a couple of starter pushes before taking her place in the game.

Alex caught the next pitch, and the ball flew high and wide. Voices erupted into shouts. Surprisingly spry, Yuri danced a few steps to the left and snagged the ball out of the air. Mikhail tagged up, streaked past third and headed for home, where Rachel had raced to wait for the throw.

His long strides ate up the ground, those wonderful muscles bunching as he went into a slide. Rachel crowded the plate, apparently undisturbed by the thought of nearly six feet of solid male hurtling toward her. There was a collision, a tangle of limbs and a great deal of swearing.

"Out." Nadia's voice rang clearly over the din.

In the majors, they called it clearing the benches.

Every member of the family rushed toward the plate—not to fuss over the two forms still nursing bruises, but to shout and gesture. Rachel punched Mikhail in the chest. He responded by covering her face with his hand and shoving her back onto the grass. With a happy shout, Brandon jumped into the fray to climb up his father's back.

Sydney had never envied anything more.

"We can never play without fighting," Natasha said from behind her. She was smiling, looking over Sydney's shoulder at the chaos in her backyard. Her arms still felt the slight weight of the baby she'd just rocked to sleep. "You're wise to watch from a distance."

But when Sydney turned, Natasha saw that her eyes were wet.

"Oh, please." Quickly she moved to Sydney's side to take her hand. "Don't be upset. They don't mean it."

"No. I know." Desperately embarrassed, she blinked the tears back. "I wasn't upset. It was just— it was silly. Watching them was something like looking at a really beautiful painting or hearing some incredibly lovely music. I got carried away."

She didn't need to say more. Natasha understood after Spence's explanation of Sydney's background that there had never been softball games, horseplay or the fun of passionate arguments in her life.

"You love him very much."

Sydney fumbled. That quiet statement wasn't as easy to respond to as Rachel's cocky question had been.

"It's not my business," Natasha continued. "But he is special to me. And I see that you're special to him. You don't find him an easy man."

"No. No, I don't."

Natasha glanced outside again, and her gaze rested on her husband, who was currently wrestling both Freddie and Brandon on the grass. Not so many years before, she thought, she'd been afraid to hope for such things.

"Does he frighten you?"

Sydney started to deny it, then found herself speaking slowly, thoughtfully. "The hugeness of his emotions sometimes frightens me. He has so many, and he finds it so easy to feel them, understand them, express them. I've never been the type to be led by mine, or swept away by them. Sometimes he just overwhelms me, and that's unnerving."

"He is what he feels," Natasha said simply. "Would you like to see some of it?" Without waiting for an answer, she walked over to a wall of shelves.

Lovely carved and painted figures danced across the shelves, some of them so tiny and exquisite it seemed impossible that any hand could have created them.

A miniature house with a gingerbread roof and candy-cane shutters, a high silver tower where a beautiful woman's golden hair streamed from the topmost window, a palm-sized canopy bed where a handsome prince knelt beside a lovely, sleeping princess.

"He brought me this one yesterday." Natasha picked up the painted figure of a woman at a spinning wheel. It sat on a tiny platform scattered with wisps of straw and specks of gold. "The miller's daughter from Rumpelstiltskin." She smiled, tracing the delicate fingertips that rode the spindle.

"They're lovely, all of them. Like a magical world of their own."

"Mikhail has magic," Natasha said. "For me, he carves fairy tales, because I learned English by reading them. Some of his work is more powerful, tragic, erotic, bold, even frightening. But it's always real, because it comes from inside him as much as from the wood or stone."

"I know. What you're trying to show me here is his sensitivity. It's not necessary. I've never known anyone more capable of kindness or compassion."

"I thought perhaps you were afraid he would hurt you."

"No," Sydney said quietly. She thought of the richness of heart it would take to create something as beautiful, as fanciful as the diminutive woman spinning straw into gold. "I'm afraid I'll hurt him."

"Sydney—" But the back door slammed and feet clambered down the hall.

The interruption relieved Sydney. Confiding her feelings was new and far from comfortable. It amazed her that she had done so with a woman she'd known less than a day.

There was something about this family, she realized. Something as magical as the fairy-tale figures Mikhail carved for his sister. Perhaps the magic was as simple as happiness.

As the afternoon wore on, they ebbed and flowed out of the house, noisy, demanding and very often dirty. Nadia eventually cleared the decks by ordering all of the men outside.

"How come they get to go out and sit in the shade with a bottle of beer while we do the cooking," Rachel grumbled as her hands worked quickly, expertly with potatoes and a peeler.

"Because..." Nadia put two dozen eggs on boil. "In here they will pick at the food, get big feet in my way and make a mess."

"Good point. Still—"

"They'll have to clean the mess we make," Natasha told her.

Satisfied, Rachel attacked another potato. Her complaints were only tokens. She was a woman who loved to cook as much as she loved trying a case. "If Vera was here, they wouldn't even do that."

"Our housekeeper," Natasha explained to Sydney while she sliced and chopped a mountain of vegetables. "She's been with us for years. We gave her the month off to take a trip with her sister. Could you wash those grapes?"

Obediently Sydney followed instructions, scrubbing fruit, fetching ingredients, stirring the occasional pot. But she knew very well that three efficient women were working around her.

"You can make deviled eggs," Nadia said kindly when she noted Sydney was at a loss. "They will be cool soon."

"I, ah . . ." She stared, marginally horrified, at the shiny white orbs she'd rinsed in the sink. "I don't know how."

"Your mama didn't teach you to cook?" It wasn't annoyance in Nadia's voice, just disbelief. Nadia had considered it her duty to teach every one of her children—whether they'd wanted to learn or not.

As far as Sydney knew, Margerite had never boiled an egg much less deviled one. Sydney offered a weak smile. "No, she taught me how to order in restaurants."

Nadia patted her cheek. "When they cool, I show you how to make them the way Mikhail likes best." She murmured in Ukrainian when Katie's waking wail came through the kitchen intercom. On impulse, Natasha shook her head before Nadia could dry her hands and go up to fetch her granddaughter.

"Sydney, would you mind?" With a guileless smile, Natasha turned to her. "My hands are full."

Sydney blinked and stared. "You want me to go get the baby?"

"Please."

More than a little uneasy, Sydney started out of the kitchen.

"What are you up to, Tash?" Rachel wanted to know.

"She wants family."

With a hoot of laughter, Rachel swung an arm around her sister and mother. "She'll get more than her share with this one."

The baby sounded very upset, Sydney thought as she hurried down the hall. She might be sick. What in the world had Natasha been thinking of not coming up to get Katie herself? Maybe when you were the mother of three, you became casual about such things. Taking a deep breath, she walked into the nursery.

Katie, her hair curling damply around her face, was hanging on to the side of the crib and howling. Unsteady legs dipped and straightened as she struggled to keep her balance. One look at Sydney had her tear-drenched face crumpling. She flung out her arms, tilted and landed on her bottom on the bright pink sheet.

"Oh, poor baby," Sydney crooned, too touched to be nervous. "Did you think no one was coming?" She picked the sniffling baby up, and Katie compensated for Sydney's awkwardness by cuddling trustingly against her body. "You're so little. Such a pretty little thing." On a shuddering sigh, Katie tipped her head back. "You look like your uncle, don't you? He got embarrassed when I said he was gorgeous, but you are."

Downstairs, three women chuckled as Sydney's voice came clearly through the intercom.

"Oh-oh." After giving the little bottom an affectionate pat, Sydney discovered a definite problem. "You're wet, right? Look, I figure your mother could handle this in about thirty seconds flat—that goes for everybody else downstairs. But everybody else isn't here. So what do we do?"

Katie had stopped sniffling and was blowing bubbles with her mouth while she tugged on Sydney's hair. "I guess we'll give it a try. I've never changed a diaper in my life," she began as she glanced around the room. "Or deviled an egg or played softball, or any damn thing. Whoops. No swearing in front of the baby. Here we go." She spotted a diaper bag in bold green stripes. "Oh, God, Katie, they're real ones."

Blowing out a breath, she took one of the neatly folded cotton diapers. "Okay, in for a penny, in for a pound. We'll just put you down on here." Gently she laid Katie on the changing table and prepared to give the operation her best shot.

"Hey." Mikhail bounded into the kitchen and was greeted by three hissing "shhs!"

"What?"

"Sydney's changing Katie," Natasha murmured and smiled at the sounds flowing through the intercom.

"Sydney?" Mikhail forgot the beer he'd been sent to fetch and stayed to listen.

"Okay, we're halfway there." Katie's little butt was dry and powdered. Perhaps a little over powdered, but better to err on the side of caution, Sydney'd figured. Her brow creased as she attempted to make the fresh diaper look like the one she'd removed, sans dampness. "This looks pretty close. What do you think?" Katie kicked her feet and giggled. "You'd be the expert. Okay, this is the tricky part. No wriggling."

Of course, she did. The more she wriggled and kicked, the more Sydney laughed and cuddled. When she'd managed to secure the diaper, Katie looked so cute, smelled so fresh, felt so soft, she had to cuddle some more. Then it seemed only right that she hold Katie up high so the baby could squeal and kick and blow more bubbles.

The diaper sagged but stayed generally where it belonged.

"Okay, gorgeous, now we're set. Want to go down and see Mama?"

"Mama," Katie gurgled, and bounced in Sydney's arms. "Mama."

In the kitchen, four people scattered and tried to look busy or casual.

"Sorry it took so long," she began as she came in. "She was wet." She saw Mikhail and stopped, her cheek pressed against Katie's.

When their eyes met, color washed to her cheeks. The muscles in her thighs went lax. It was no way, no way at all, she thought, for him to be looking at her with his mother and sisters in the room.

"I'll take her." Stepping forward, he held out his arms. Katie stretched into them. Still watching Sydney, he rubbed his cheek over the baby's head and settled her with a natural ease on his hip. "Come here." Before Sydney could respond, he cupped a hand behind her head and pulled her against him for a long, blood-thumping kiss. Well used to such behavior, Katie only bounced and gurgled.

Slowly he slid away, then smiled at her. "I'll come back for the beer." Juggling Katie, he swaggered out, slamming the screen door behind him.

"Now." Nadia took a dazed Sydney by the hands. "You make deviled eggs."

The sun was just setting on the weekend when Sydney unlocked the door of her apartment. She was laughing—and she was sure she'd laughed more in two days than she had in her entire life. She set the packages she carried on the sofa as Mikhail kicked the door closed.

"You put more in here to come back than you had when you left," he accused, and set her suitcase down.

"One or two things." Smiling, she walked over to slip her arms around his waist. It felt good, wonderfully good, especially knowing that his would circle her in response. *"Dyakuyu,"* she said, sampling *thank you* in his language.

"You mangle it, but you're welcome." He kissed both her cheeks. *"This* is the traditional greeting or farewell."

She had to bite the tip of her tongue to hold back the grin. "I know." She also knew why he was telling her—again. She'd been kissed warmly by each member of the family. Not the careless touch of cheek to cheek she was accustomed to, but a firm pressure of lips, accompanied by a full-blooded embrace. Only Alex hadn't settled for her cheeks.

"Your brother kisses very well." Eyes as solemn as she could manage, Sydney touched her lips to Mikhail's cheeks in turn. "It must run in the family."

"You liked it?"

"Well..." She shot Mikhail a look from under her lashes. "He did have a certain style."

"He's a boy," Mikhail muttered, though Alex was less than two years his junior.

"Oh, no." This time a quick laugh bubbled out. "He's definitely not a boy. But I think you have a marginal advantage."

"Marginal."

She linked her hands comfortably behind his neck. "As a carpenter, you'd know that even a fraction of an inch can be vital—for fit."

His hands snagged her hips to settle her against him. "So, I fit you, Hayward?"

"Yes." She smiled as he touched his lips to her brow. "It seems you do."

"And you like my kisses better than Alex's?"

She sighed, enjoying the way his mouth felt skimming down her temples, over her jaw. "Marginally." Her eyes flew open when he pinched her. "Well, really—"

But that was all she managed to get out before his mouth closed over hers. She thought of flash fires, ball lightning and electrical overloads. With a murmur of approval, she tossed heat back at him.

"Now." Instantly aroused, he scooped her up in his arms. "I suppose I must prove myself."

Sydney hooked her arms around his neck. "If you insist."

A dozen long strides and he was in the bedroom, where he dropped her unceremoniously onto the bed. By the time she had her breath back, he'd yanked off his shirt and shoes.

"What are you grinning at?" he demanded.

"It's that pirate look again." Still smiling, she brushed hair out of her eyes. "All you need is a saber and a black patch."

He hooked his thumbs in frayed belt loops. "So, you think I'm a barbarian."

She let her gaze slide up his naked torso, over the wild mane of hair, the stubble that proved he hadn't bothered to pack a razor for the weekend. To his eyes, those dark, dramatic, dangerous eyes. "I think you're dazzling."

He would have winced but she looked so small and pretty, sitting on the bed, her hair tumbled from the wind, her face still flushed from his rough, impatient kiss.

He remembered how she'd looked, walking into the kitchen, carrying Katie. Her eyes had been full of delight and wonder and shyness. She'd flushed when his mother had announced that Sydney had made the eggs herself. And again, when his father had wrapped her in a bear hug. But Mikhail had seen that she'd hung on, that her fingers had curled into Yuri's shirt, just for an instant.

There were dozens of other flashes of memory. How she'd snuggled the puppy or taken Brandon's hand or stroked Freddie's hair.

She needed love. She was strong and smart and sensible. And she needed love.

Frowning, he sat on the edge of the bed and took her hand. Uneasiness skidded down Sydney's spine.

"What is it? What did I do wrong?"

It wasn't the first time he'd heard that strain of insecurity and doubt in her voice. Biting back the questions and the impatience, he shook his head. "Nothing. It's me." Turning her hand over, he pressed a soft kiss in the center of her palm, then to her wrist where her pulse was beating as quickly from fear as from arousal. "I forget to be gentle with you. To be tender."

She'd hurt his feelings. His ego. She hadn't been responsive enough. Too responsive. Oh, God. "Mikhail, I was only teasing about Alex. I wasn't complaining."

"Maybe you should."

"No." Shifting to her knees, she threw her arms around him and pressed her lips to his. "I want you," she said desperately. "You know how much I want you."

Even as the fire leaped in his gut, he brought his hands lightly to her face, fingers stroking easily. The emotion he poured into the kiss came from the heart only and was filled with sweetness, with kindness, with love.

For a moment, she struggled for the heat, afraid she might never find it. But his mouth was so soft, so patient. As her urgency turned to wonder, his lips rubbed over hers. And the friction sparked not the familiar flash fire, but a warm glow, golden, so quietly beautiful her throat ached with it. Even when he took the kiss deeper, deeper, there was only tenderness. Weakened by it, her body melted like wax. Her hands slid limp and useless from his shoulders in total surrender.

"Beautiful. So beautiful," he murmured as he laid her back on the bed, emptying her mind, stirring her soul with long, drowning kisses. "I should be shot for showing you only one way."

"I can't..." Think, breathe, move.

"Shh." Gently, with an artist's touch, he undressed her. "Tonight is only for you. Only to enjoy." His breath caught as the dying sunlight glowed over her skin. She looked too fragile to touch. Too lovely not to. "Let me show you what you are to me."

Everything. She was everything. After tonight he wanted her to have no doubt of it. With slow, worshipful hands, he showed her that beyond passion, beyond desire, was a merging of spirits. A generosity of the soul.

Love could be peaceful, selfless, enduring.

Her body was a banquet, fragrant, dazzling with erotic flavors. But tonight, he sampled slowly, savoring, sharing. Each sigh, each shudder filled him with gratitude that she was his.

He wouldn't allow her to race. Helpless to resist, she floated down the long, dark river where he guided her through air the essence of silk. Never, not even during their most passionate joining, had she been so aware of her own body. Her own texture and shape and scent. And his. Oh, Lord, and his.

Those rock-hard muscles and brute strength now channeled into unimagined gentleness. The subtlety of movement elicited new longings, fresh knowledge and a symphony of understanding that was exquisite in its harmony.

Let me give you. Let me show you. Let me take.

Sensitive fingertips traced over her, lingering to arouse, moving on to seek out some new shattering pleasure. And from her pleasure came his own, just as sweet, just as staggering, just as simple.

She could hear her own breathing, a quiet, trembling sound as the room deepened with night. A tribute to beauty, tears dampened her cheeks and thickened her voice when she spoke his name.

His mouth covered hers again as at last he slipped inside her. Enfolded in her, cradled by her, he trembled under the long, sighing sweep of sensation. Her mouth opened beneath his, her arms lifted, circled, held.

More. He remembered that he had once fought desperately for more. Now, with her, he had all.

Even with hot hammers of need pounding at him, he moved slowly, knowing he could take her soaring again and again before that last glorious release.

"I love you, Sydney." His muscles trembled as he felt her rise to meet him. "Only you. Always you."

Chapter Eleven

When the phone rang, it was pitch-dark and they were sleeping, tangled together like wrestling children. Sydney snuggled closer to Mikhail, squeezing her eyes tighter and muttered a single no, determined to ignore it.

With a grunt, Mikhail rolled over her, seriously considered staying just as he was as her body curved deliciously to his.

"*Milaya,*" he murmured, then with an oath, snatched the shrilling phone off the hook.

"What?" Because Sydney was pounding on his shoulder, he shifted off her. "Alexi?" The sound of his brother's voice had him sitting straight up, firing off in Ukrainian. Only when Alex assured him there was nothing wrong with the family did the sick panic fade. "You'd better be in the hospital or jail. Nei-

ther?'' He sat back, rapped his head on the brass poles
of the headboard and swore again. ''Why are you
calling in the middle of the night?'' Rubbing his hand
over his face, Mikhail gave Sydney's clock a vicious
stare. The glowing dial read 4:45. ''What?'' Struggling to tune in, he shifted the phone to his other ear.
''Damn it, when? I'll be there.''

He slammed the phone down and was already up
searching for his clothes when he realized Sydney has
turned on the light. Her face was dead pale.

''Your parents.''

''No, no, it's not the family.'' He sat on the bed
again to take her hand. ''It's the apartment. Vandals.''

The sharp edge of fear dulled to puzzlement.
''Vandals?''

''One of the cops who answered the call knows
Alex, and that I live there, so he called him. There's
been some damage.''

''To the building.'' Her heart was beginning to
pound, heavy and slow, in her throat.

''Yes, no one was hurt.'' He watched her eyes close
in relief at that before she nodded. ''Spray paint, broken windows.'' He bit off an oath. ''Two of the empty
apartments were flooded. I'm going to go see what has
to be done.''

''Give me ten minutes,'' Sydney said and sprang out
of bed.

It hurt. It was only brick and wood and glass, but it
hurt her to see it marred. Filthy obscenities were
scrawled in bright red paint across the lovely old
brownstone. Three of the lower windows were shat-

tered. Inside, someone had used a knife to gouge the railings and hack at the plaster.

In Mrs. Wolburg's apartment water was three inches deep over the old hardwood floor, ruining her rugs, soaking the skirts of her sofa. Her lacy doilies floated like soggy lily pads.

"They clogged up the sinks," Alex explained. "By the time they broke the windows downstairs and woke anyone up, the damage here was pretty much done."

Yes, the damage was done, Sydney thought. But it wasn't over. "The other unit?"

"Up on two. Empty. They did a lot of painting up there, too." He gave Sydney's arm a squeeze. "I'm sorry. We're getting statements from the tenants, but—"

"It was dark," Sydney finished. "Everyone was asleep, and no one's going to have seen anything."

"Nothing's impossible." Alex turned toward the babble of voices coming from the lobby, where most of the tenants had gathered. "Why don't you go on up to Mikhail's place? It's going to take a while to calm everyone down and clear them out."

"No, it's my building. I'd like to go talk to them."

With a nod, he started to lead her down the hall. "Funny they didn't bother to steal anything—and that they only broke into the two empty apartments."

She slanted him a look. He might not have been wearing his uniform, but he was definitely a cop. "Is this an interrogation, Alex?"

"Just an observation. I guess you'd know who had access to the tenants' list."

"I guess I would," she replied. "I have a pretty fair idea who's responsible, Alex." She touched a hand to the ruined banister. "Oh, not who tossed paint or flooded the rooms, but who arranged it. But I don't know if I'll be able to prove it."

"You leave the proving up to us."

She glanced at the streak of paint along the wall. "Would you?" She shook her head before he could reply. "Once I'm sure, I'll turn everything over to you. That's a promise—if you promise to say nothing to Mikhail."

"That's a tough bargain, Sydney."

"I'm a tough lady," she said steadily, and walked down to talk to her tenants.

By eight o'clock she was in her office poring over every word in Lloyd Bingham's personnel file. By ten, she'd made several phone calls, consumed too many cups of coffee and had a structured plan.

She'd authorized Mikhail to hire more men, had spoken with the insurance investigator personally and was now prepared for a little psychological warfare.

She put the call through to Lloyd Bingham herself and waited three rings.

"Hello."

"Lloyd, Sydney Hayward."

She heard the rasp of a lighter. "Got a problem?"

"Not that can't be fixed. It was really a very pitiful gesture, Lloyd."

"I don't know what you're talking about."

"Of course you don't." The sarcasm was brisk, almost careless. "Next time, I'd suggest you do more thorough research."

"You want to come to the point?"

"The point is my building, my tenants and your mistake."

"It's a little early in the day for puzzles." The smug satisfaction in his voice had her fingers curling.

"It's not a puzzle when the solution is so clear. I don't imagine you were aware of just how many service people live in the building. And how early some of those service people get up in the morning, have their coffee, glance out the window. Or how cooperative those people would be in giving descriptions to the police."

"If something happened to your building, that's your problem." He drew hard on his cigarette. "I haven't been near it."

"I never thought you had been," she said easily. "You've always been good at delegating. But once certain parties are picked up by the police, I think you'll discover how unsettling it is not to have loyal employees."

She could have sworn she heard him sweat. "I don't have to listen to this."

"No, of course you don't. And I won't keep you. Oh, Lloyd, don't let them talk you into a bonus. They didn't do a very thorough job. Ciao."

She hung up, immensely satisfied. If she knew her quarry, he wouldn't wait long to meet with his hirelings and pay them off. And since the investigator had been very interested in Sydney's theory, she doubted that meeting would go unobserved.

She flicked her intercom. "Janine, I need food before we start interviewing the new secretaries. Order anything the deli says looks good today and double it."

"You got it. I was about to buzz you, Sydney. Your mother's here."

The little bubble of success burst in her throat. "Tell her I'm . . ." *Coward.* "No, tell her to come in." But she took a deep breath before she rose and walked to the door. "Mother."

"Sydney, dear." Lovely in ivory linen and smelling of Paris, she strolled in and bussed Sydney's cheek. "I'm so sorry."

"I—what?"

"I've had to wait all weekend to contact you and apologize." Margerite took a steadying breath herself, twisting her envelope bag in her hands. "May I sit?"

"Of course. I'm sorry. Would you like anything?"

"To completely erase Friday evening from my life." Seated, Margerite gave her daughter an embarrassed glance. "This isn't easy for me, Sydney. The simple fact is, I was jealous."

"Oh, Mother."

"No, please." Margerite waved her daughter to the chair beside her. "I don't enjoy the taste of crow and hope you'll let me get it done in one large swallow."

As embarrassed as her mother, Sydney sat and reached for her hand. "It isn't necessary that you swallow at all. We'll just forget it."

Margerite shook her head. "I hope I'm big enough to admit my failings. I like thinking I'm still an attractive and desirable woman."

"You are."

Margerite smiled fleetingly. "But certainly not an admirable one when I find myself eaten up with envy to see that a man I'd hoped to, well, enchant, was instead enchanted by my daughter. I regret, very much, my behavior and my words. There," she said on a puff of breath. "Will you forgive me?"

"Of course I will. And I'll apologize, too, for speaking to you the way I did."

Margerite took a little square of lace from her bag and dabbed at her eyes. "You surprised me, I admit. I've never seen you so passionate about anything. He's a beautiful man, dear. I won't say I approve of a relationship between you, but I can certainly understand it." She sighed as she tucked the handkerchief back into her bag. "Your happiness is important to me, Sydney."

"I know that."

Her eyes still glistened when she looked at her daughter. "I'm so glad we cleared the air. And I want to do something for you, something to make up for all of this."

"You don't have to do anything."

"I want to, really. Have dinner with me tonight."

Sydney thought of the dozens of things she had to do, of the quiet meal she'd hoped for at the end of it all with Mikhail. Then she looked at her mother's anxious eyes. "I'd love to."

"Wonderful." The spring was back in her step as Margerite got to her feet. "Eight o'clock. Le Cirque." She gave Sydney a quick and genuine hug before she strolled out.

By eight, Sydney would have preferred a long, solitary nap, but stepped from her car dressed for the evening in a sleeveless silk jumpsuit of icy blue.

"My mother's driver will take me home, Donald."

"Very good, Ms. Hayward. Enjoy your evening."

"Thank you."

The maître d' recognized her the moment she walked in and gracefully led her to her table himself. As she passed through the elegant restaurant filled with sparkling people and exotic scents, she imagined Mikhail, sitting at his scarred workbench with a bottle of beer and a bowl of goulash.

She tried not to sigh in envy.

When she spotted her mother—with Channing—at the corner table, she tried not to grit her teeth.

"There you are, darling." So certain her surprise was just what her daughter needed, Margerite didn't notice the lights of war in Sydney's eyes. "Isn't this lovely?"

"Lovely." Sydney's voice was flat as Channing rose to pull out her chair. She said nothing when he bent close to kiss her cheek.

"You look beautiful tonight, Sydney."

The champagne was already chilled and open. She waited while hers was poured, but the first sip did nothing to clear the anger from her throat. "Mother didn't mention you'd be joining us tonight."

"That was my surprise," Margerite bubbled like the wine in her glass. "My little make-up present." Following a prearranged signal, she set her napkin aside and rose. "I'm sure you two will excuse me while I powder my nose."

Knowing he only had fifteen minutes to complete his mission, Channing immediately took Sydney's hand. "I've missed you, darling. It seems like weeks since I've had a moment alone with you."

Skillfully Sydney slipped her hand from him. "It has been weeks. How have you been, Channing?"

"Desolate without you." He skimmed a fingertip up her bare arm. She really had exquisite skin. "When are we going to stop playing these games, Sydney?"

"I haven't been playing." She took a sip of wine. "I've been working."

A trace of annoyance clouded his eyes then cleared. He was sure Margerite was right. Once they were married, she would be too busy with him to bother with a career. It was best to get right to the point. "Darling, we've been seeing each other for months now. And of course, we've known each other for years. But things have changed."

She met his eyes. "Yes, they have."

Encouraged, he took her hand again. "I haven't wanted to rush you, but I feel it's time we take the next step. I care for you very much, Sydney. I find you lovely and amusing and sweet."

"And suitable," she muttered.

"Of course. I want you to be my wife." He slipped a box from his pocket, opened the lid so that the round icy diamond could flash in the candlelight.

"Channing—"

"It reminded me of you," he interrupted. "Regal and elegant."

"It's beautiful, Channing," she said carefully. And cold, she thought. So very cold. "And I'm sorry, but I can't accept it. Or you."

Shock came first, then a trickle of annoyance. "Sydney, we're both adults. There's no need to be coy."

"What I'm trying to be is honest." She shifted in her chair, and this time it was she who took his hands. "I can't tell you how sorry I am that my mother led you to believe I'd feel differently. By doing so, she's put us both in an embarrassing position. Let's be candid, Channing. You don't love me, and I don't love you."

Insulted, he pokered up. "I hardly think I'd be offering marriage otherwise."

"You're offering it because you find me attractive, you think I'd make an excellent hostess, and because I come from the same circle as you. Those are reasons for a merger, not a marriage." She closed the lid on the diamond and pressed the box into his hands. "I make a poor wife, Channing, that much I know. And I have no intention of becoming one again."

He relaxed a little. "I understand you might still be a bit raw over what happened between you and Peter."

"No, you don't understand at all what happened between me and Peter. To be honest, that has nothing to do with my refusing you. I don't love you, Channing, and I'm very much in love with someone else."

His fair skin flushed dark red. "Then I find it worse than insulting that you would pretend an affection for me."

"I do have an affection for you," she said wearily. "But that's all I have. I can only apologize if I failed to make that clear before this."

"I don't believe an apology covers it, Sydney." Stiffly he rose to his feet. "Please give my regrets to your mother."

Straight as a poker, he strode out, leaving Sydney alone with a miserable mix of temper and guilt. Five minutes later, Margerite came out of the ladies' room, beaming. "Well now." She leaned conspiratorially toward her daughter, pleased to see that Channing had given them a few moments alone. "Tell me everything."

"Channing's gone, Mother."

"Gone?" Bright eyed, Margerite glanced around. "What do you mean gone?"

"I mean he's left, furious, I might add, because I declined his proposal of marriage."

"Declined?" Margerite blinked. "You— Sydney, how could you?"

"How could I?" Her voice rose and, catching herself, she lowered it to a whisper. "How could you? You set this entire evening up."

"Of course I did." Frazzled, Margerite waved the oncoming waiter away and reached for her wine. "I've planned for months to see you and Channing together. And since it was obvious that Mikhail had brought you out of your shell, the timing was perfect. Channing is exactly what you need. He's eligible, his family is above reproach, he has a beautiful home and excellent bearing."

"I don't love him."

"Sydney, for heaven's sake, be sensible."

"I've never been anything else, and perhaps that's been the problem. I believed you when you came to see me this morning. I believed you were sorry, that you cared, and that you wanted something more than polite words between us."

Margerite's eyes filled. "Everything I said this morning was true. I'd been miserable all weekend, thinking I'd driven you away. You're my daughter, I do care. I want what's best for you."

"You mean it," Sydney murmured, suddenly, unbearably weary. "But you also believe that you know what's best for me. I don't mean to hurt you, but I've come to understand you've never known what's best for me. By doing this tonight, you caused me to hurt Channing in a way I never meant to."

A tear spilled over. "Sydney, I only thought—"

"Don't think for me." She was perilously close to tears herself. "Don't ever think for me again. I let you do that before, and I ruined someone's life."

"I don't want you to be alone," Margerite choked out. "It's hateful being alone."

"Mother." Though she was afraid she might weaken too much, too soon, she took Margerite's hands. "Listen to me, listen carefully. I love you, but I can't be you. I want to know that we can have an honest, caring relationship. It'll take time. But it can't ever happen unless you try to understand me, unless you respect me for who I am, and not for what you want me to be. I can't marry Channing to please you. I can't marry anyone."

"Oh, Sydney."

"There are things you don't know. Things I don't want to talk about. Just please trust me. I know what I'm doing. I've been happier in the last few weeks than I've ever been."

"Stanislaski," Margerite said on a sigh.

"Yes, Stanislaski. And Hayward," she added. "And me. I'm doing something with my life, Mother. It's making a difference. Now let's go fix your makeup and start over."

* * *

At his workbench, Mikhail polished the rosewood bust. He hadn't meant to work so late, but Sydney had simply emerged in his hands. There was no way to explain the way it felt to have her come to life there. It wasn't powerful. It was humbling. He'd barely had to think. Though his fingers were cramped, proving how long he had carved and sanded and polished, he could barely remember the technique he'd used.

The tools didn't matter, only the result. Now she was there with him, beautiful, warm, alive. And he knew it was a piece he would never part with.

Sitting back, he circled his shoulders to relieve the stiffness. It had been a viciously long day, starting before dawn. He'd had to channel the edge of his rage into organizing the cleaning up and repair the worst of the damage. Now that the impetus that had driven him to complete the bust was passed, he was punchy with fatigue. But he didn't want to go to bed. An empty bed.

How could he miss her so much after only hours? Why did it feel as though she were a world away when she was only at the other end of the city? He wasn't going to go through another night without her, he vowed as he stood up to pace. She was going to have to understand that. He would make her understand that. A woman had no right to make herself vital to a man's existence then leave him restless and alone at midnight.

Dragging a hand through his hair, he considered his options. He could go to bed and will himself to sleep. He could call her and satisfy himself with the sound of her voice. Or he could go uptown and beat on her door until she let him in.

He grinned, liking the third choice best. Snatching up a shirt, he tugged it on as he headed for the door. Sydney gave a surprised gasp as he yanked it open just as her hand was poised to knock.

"Oh. What instincts." She pressed the hand to her heart. "I'm sorry to come by so late, but I saw your light was on, so I—"

He didn't let her finish, but pulled her inside and held her until she wondered her ribs didn't crack. "I was coming for you," he muttered.

"Coming for me? I just left the restaurant."

"I wanted you. I wanted to—" He broke off and snapped her back. "It's after midnight. What are you doing coming all the way downtown after midnight?"

"For heaven's sake—"

"It's not safe for a woman alone."

"I was perfectly safe."

He shook his head, cupping her chin. "Next time, you call. I'll come to you." Then his eyes narrowed. An artist's eyes, a lover's eyes saw beyond carefully repaired makeup. "You've been crying."

There was such fury in the accusation, she had to laugh. "No, not really. Mother got a bit emotional, and there was a chain reaction."

"I thought you said you'd made up with her."

"I did. I have. At least I think we've come to a better understanding."

He smiled a little, tracing a finger over Sydney's lips. "She does not approve of me for her daughter."

"That's not really the problem. I'm afraid she's feeling a little worn down. She had her plans blow up in her face tonight."

"You'll tell me."

"Yes." She walked over, intending to collapse on his badly sprung couch. But she saw the bust. Slowly she moved closer to study it. When she spoke, her voice was low and thick. "You have an incredible talent."

"I carve what I see, what I know, what I feel."

"Is this how you see me?"

"It's how you are." He laid his hands lightly on her shoulders. "For me."

Then she was beautiful for him, Sydney thought. And she was trembling with life and love, for him. "I didn't even pose for you."

"You will." He brushed his lips over her hair. "Talk to me."

"When I met Mother at the restaurant, Channing was with her."

Over Sydney's head, Mikhail's eyes darkened dangerously. "The banker with the silk suits. You let him kiss you before you let me."

"I knew him before I knew you." Amused, Sydney turned and looked jealousy in the eye. "And I didn't let you kiss me, as I recall. You just did."

He did so again, ruthlessly. "You won't let him again."

"No."

"Good." He drew her to the sofa. "Then he can live."

With a laugh, she threw her arms around him for a hug, then settled her head on his shoulder. "None of it's his fault, really. Or my mother's, either. It's more a matter of habit and circumstance. She'd set up the evening after persuading Channing that the time was ripe to propose.''

''Propose?'' Mikhail spun her around to face him. ''He wants to marry you?''

''Not really. He thought he did. He certainly doesn't want to marry me anymore.'' But he was shoving her out of the way so he could get up and pace. ''There's no reason to be angry,'' Sydney said as she smoothed down her jumpsuit. ''I was the one in the awkward position. As it is I doubt he'll speak to me again.''

''If he does, I'll cut out his tongue.'' Slowly, Mikhail thought, working up the rage. ''No one marries you but me.''

''I've already explained…'' She trailed off as breath lodged in a hard ball in her throat. ''There's really no need to go into this,'' she managed as she rose. ''It's late.''

''You wait,'' Mikhail ordered and strode into the bedroom. When he came back carrying a small box, Sydney's blood turned to ice. ''Sit.''

''No, Mikhail, please—''

''Then stand.'' He flipped open the top of the box to reveal a ring of hammered gold with a small center stone of fiery red. ''The grandfather of my father made this for his wife. He was a goldsmith so the work is fine, even though the stone is small. It comes to me because I am the oldest son. If it doesn't please you, I buy you something else.''

''No, it's beautiful. Please, don't. I can't.'' She held her fisted hands behind her back. ''Don't ask me.''

''I am asking you,'' he said impatiently. ''Give me your hand.''

She took a step back. "I can't wear the ring. I can't marry you."

With a shake of his head, he pulled her hand free and pushed the ring on her finger. "See, you can wear it. It's too big, but we'll fix it."

"No." She would have pulled it off again, but he closed his hand over hers. "I don't want to marry you."

His fingers tightened on hers, and a fire darted into his eyes, more brilliant than the shine of the ruby. "Why?"

"I don't want to get married," she said as clearly as she could. "I won't have what we started together spoiled."

"Marriage doesn't spoil love, it nurtures it."

"You don't know," she snapped back. "You've never been married. I have. And I won't go through it again."

"So." Struggling with temper, he rocked back on his heels. "This husband of yours hurt you, makes you unhappy, so you think I'll do the same."

"Damn it, I loved him." Her voice broke, and she covered her face with her hand as the tears began to fall.

Torn between jealousy and misery, he gathered her close, murmuring endearments as he stroked her hair. "I'm sorry."

"You don't understand."

"Let me understand." He tilted her face up to kiss the tears. "I'm sorry," he repeated. "I won't yell at you anymore."

"It's not that." She let out a shuddering breath. "I don't want to hurt you. Please, let this go."

"I can't let this go. Or you. I love you, Sydney. I need you. For my life I need you. Explain to me why you won't take me."

"If there was anyone," she began in a rush, then shook her head before she could even wish it. "Mikhail, I can't consider marriage. Hayward is too much of a responsibility, and I need to focus on my career."

"This is smoke, to hide the real answer."

"All right." Bracing herself, she stepped away from him. "I don't think I could handle failing again, and losing someone I love. Marriage changes people."

"How did it change you?"

"I loved Peter, Mikhail. Not the way I love you, but more than anyone else. He was my best friend. We grew up together. When my parents divorced, he was the only one I could talk to. He cared, really cared, about how I felt, what I thought, what I wanted. We could sit for hours on the beach up at the Hamptons and watch the water, tell each other secrets."

She turned away. Saying it all out loud brought the pain spearing back.

"And you fell in love."

"No," she said miserably. "We just loved each other. I can hardly remember a time without him. And I can't remember when it started to become a given that we'd marry someday. Not that we talked about it ourselves. Everyone else did. Sydney and Peter, what a lovely couple they make. Isn't it nice how well they suit? I suppose we heard it so much, we started to believe it. Anyway, it was expected, and we'd both been raised to do what was expected of us."

She brushed at tears and wandered over to his shelves. "You were right when you gave me that figure of Cinderella. I've always followed the rules. I was expected to go to boarding school and get top grades. So I did. I was expected to behave presentably, never to show unacceptable emotions. So I did. I was expected to marry Peter. So I did."

She whirled back. "There we were, both of us just turned twenty-two—quite an acceptable age for marriage. I suppose we both thought it would be fine. After all, we'd known each other forever, we liked the same things, understood each other. Loved each other. But it wasn't fine. Almost from the beginning. Honeymooning in Greece. We both loved the country. And we both pretended that the physical part of marriage was fine. Of course, it was anything but fine, and the more we pretended, the further apart we became. We moved back to New York so he could take his place in the family business. I decorated the house, gave parties. And dreaded watching the sun go down."

"It was a mistake," Mikhail said gently.

"Yes, it was. One I made, one I was responsible for. I lost my closest friend, and before it was over, all the love was gone. There were only arguments and accusations. I was frigid, why shouldn't he have turned to someone else for a little warmth? But we kept up appearances. That was expected. And when we divorced, we did so in a very cold, very controlled, very civilized manner. I couldn't be a wife to him, Mikhail."

"It's not the same for us." He went to her.

"No, it's not. And I won't let it be."

"You're hurt because of something that happened to you, not something you did." He caught her face in his hands when she shook her head. "Yes. You need to let go of it, and trust what we have. I'll give you time."

"No." Desperate, she clamped her hands on his wrists. "Don't you see it's the same thing? You love me, so you expect me to marry you, because that's what you want—what you think is best."

"Not best," he said, giving her a quick shake. "Right. I need to share my life with you. I want to live with you, make babies with you. Watch them grow. There's a family inside us, Sydney."

She jerked away. He wouldn't listen, she thought. He wouldn't understand. "Marriage and family aren't in my plans," she said, suddenly cold. "You're going to have to accept that."

"Accept? You love me. I'm good enough for that. Good enough for you to take to your bed, but not for changing plans. All because you once followed rules instead of your heart."

"What I'm following now is my common sense." She walked by him to the door. "I'm sorry, I can't give you what you want."

"You will not go home alone."

"I think it'll be better if I leave."

"You want to leave, you leave." He stalked over to wrench the door open. "But I'll take you."

It wasn't until she lay teary and fretful in her bed that she realized she still wore his ring.

Chapter Twelve

It wasn't that she buried herself in work over the next two days, it was that work buried her. Sydney only wished it had helped. Keeping busy was supposed to be good for the morale. So why was hers flat on its face?

She closed the biggest deal of her career at Hayward, hired a new secretary to take the clerical weight off Janine and handled a full-staff meeting. Hayward stock had climbed three full points in the past ten days. The board was thrilled with her.

And she was miserable.

"An Officer Stanislaski on two, Ms. Hayward," her new secretary said through the intercom.

"Stan—oh." Her spirits did a jig, then settled. *Officer.* "Yes, I'll take it. Thank you." Sydney pasted on a smile for her own peace of mind. "Alex?"

"Hey, pretty lady. Thought you'd want to be the first to know. They just brought your old pal Lloyd Bingham in for questioning."

Her smiled faded. "I see."

"The insurance investigator took your advice and kept an eye on him. He met with a couple of bad numbers yesterday, passed some bills. Once they were picked up, they sang better than Springsteen."

"Then Lloyd did hire someone to vandalize the building."

"So they say. I don't think you're going to have any trouble from him for a while."

"I'm glad to hear it."

"You were pretty sharp, homing in on him. Brains and beauty," he said with a sigh that nearly made her smile again. "Why don't we take off to Jamaica for a couple of days? Drive Mikhail crazy?"

"I think he's already mad enough."

"Hey, he's giving you a hard time? Just come to Uncle Alex." When she didn't respond, the teasing note dropped out of his voice. "Don't mind Mik, Sydney. He's got moods, that's all. It's the artist. He's nuts about you."

"I know." Her fingers worried the files on her desk. "Maybe you could give him a call, tell him the news."

"Sure. Anything else you want me to pass on?"

"Tell him . . . no," she decided. "No, I've already told him. Thanks for calling, Alex."

"No problem. Let me know if you change your mind about Jamaica."

She hung up, wishing she felt as young as Alex had sounded. As happy. As easy. But then Alex wasn't in love. And he hadn't punched a hole in his own dreams.

Is that what she'd done? Sydney wondered as she pushed away from her desk. Had she sabotaged her own yearnings? No, she'd stopped herself, and the man she loved from making a mistake. Marriage wasn't always the answer. She had her own example to prove it. And her mother's. Once Mikhail had cooled off, he'd accept her position, and they could go on as they had before.

Who was she kidding?

He was too stubborn, too bullheaded, too damn sure his way was the right way to back down for an instant.

And what if he said all or nothing? What would she do then? Snatching up a paper clip, she began to twist it as she paced the office. If it was a matter of giving him up and losing him, or giving in and risking losing him...

God, she needed someone to talk to. Since it couldn't be Mikhail, she was left with pitifully few choices. Once she would have taken her problems to Peter, but that was...

She stopped, snapping the mangled metal in her fingers. That was the source of the problem. And maybe, just maybe, the solution.

Without giving herself time to think, she rushed out of her office and into Janine's. "I have to leave town for a couple of days," she said without preamble.

Janine was already rising from behind her new desk. "But—"

"I know it's sudden, and inconvenient, but it can't be helped. There's nothing vital pending at the moment, so you should be able to handle whatever comes in. If you can't, then it has to wait."

"Sydney, you have three appointments tomorrow."

"You take them. You have the files, you have my viewpoint. As soon as I get to where I'm going, I'll call in."

"But, Sydney." Janine scurried to the door as Sydney strode away. "Where are you going?"

"To see an old friend."

Less than an hour after Sydney had rushed from her office, Mikhail stormed in. He'd had it. He'd given the woman two days to come to her senses, and she was out of time. They were going to have this out and have it out now.

He breezed by the new secretary with a curt nod and pushed open Sydney's door.

"Excuse me. Sir, excuse me."

Mikhail whirled on the hapless woman. "Where the hell is she?"

"Ms. Hayward is not in the office," she said primly. "I'm afraid you'll have to—"

"If not here, where?"

"I'll handle this, Carla," Janine murmured from the doorway.

"Yes, ma'am." Carla made her exit quickly and with relief.

"Ms. Hayward's not here, Mr. Stanislaski. Is there something I can do for you?"

"Tell me where she is."

"I'm afraid I can't." The look in his eyes had her backing up a step. "I only know she's out of town for a day or two. She left suddenly and didn't tell me where she was going."

"Out of town?" He scowled at the empty desk, then back at Janine. "She doesn't leave her work like this."

"I admit it's unusual. But I got the impression it was important. I'm sure she'll call in. I'll be happy to give her a message for you."

He said something short and hard in Ukrainian and stormed out again.

"I think I'd better let you tell her that yourself," Janine murmured to the empty room.

Twenty-four hours after leaving her office, Sydney stood on a shady sidewalk in Georgetown, Washington, D.C. A headlong rush of adrenaline had brought her this far, far enough to have her looking at the home where Peter had settled when he'd relocated after the divorce.

The impulsive drive to the airport, the quick shuttle from city to city had been easy enough. Even the phone call to request an hour of Peter's time hadn't been so difficult. But this, this last step was nearly impossible.

She hadn't seen him in over three years, and then it had been across a wide table in a lawyer's office. Civilized, God, yes, they'd been civilized. And strangers.

It was foolish, ridiculous, taking off on this kind of tangent. Talking to Peter wouldn't change anything. Nothing could. Yet she found herself climbing the stairs to the porch of the lovely old row house, lifting the brass knocker and letting it rap on the door.

He answered himself, looking so much the same that she nearly threw out her hands to him as she would have done once. He was tall and leanly built, elegantly casual in khakis and a linen shirt. His sandy hair was attractively rumpled. But the green eyes didn't light with pleasure, instead remaining steady and cool.

"Sydney," he said, backing up to let her inside.

The foyer was cool and light, speaking subtly in its furnishings and artwork of discreet old money. "I appreciate you seeing me like this, Peter."

"You said it was important."

"To me."

"Well, then." Knowing nothing else to say, he ushered her down the hall and into a sitting room. Manners sat seamlessly on both of them, causing her to make the right comments about the house, and him to parry them while offering her a seat and a drink.

"You're enjoying Washington, then."

"Very much." He sipped his own wine while she simply turned her glass around and around in her hand. She was nervous. He knew her too well not to recognize the signs. And she was as lovely as ever. It hurt. He hated the fact that it hurt just to look at her. And the best way to get past the pain was to get to the point.

"What is it I can do for you, Sydney?"

Strangers, she thought again as she looked down at her glass. They had known each other all of their lives, had been married for nearly three years, and were strangers. "It's difficult to know where to start."

He leaned back in his chair and gestured. "Pick a spot."

"Peter, why did you marry me?"

"I beg your pardon."

"I want to know why you married me."

Whatever he'd been expecting, it hadn't been this. Shifting, he drank again. "For several of the usual reasons, I suppose."

"You loved me?"

His eyes flashed to hers. "You know I loved you."

"I know we loved each other. You were my friend." She pressed her lips together. "My best friend."

He got up to pour more wine. "We were children."

"Not when we married. We were young, but we weren't children. And we were still friends. I don't know how it all went so wrong, Peter, or what I did to ruin it so completely, but—"

"You?" He stared, the bottle in one hand, the glass in the other. "What do you mean *you* ruined it?"

"I made you unhappy, miserably unhappy. I know I failed in bed, and it all spilled over into the rest until you couldn't even bear to be around me."

"You didn't want me to touch you," he shot back. "Damn it, it was like making love to—"

"An iceberg," she finished flatly. "So you said."

Fighting guilt, he set his glass down. "I said a lot of things, so did you. I thought I'd gotten past most of it until I heard your voice this afternoon."

"I'm sorry." She rose, her body and voice stiff to compensate for shattered pride. "I've just made it worse coming here. I am sorry, Peter, I'll go."

"It was like making love with my sister." The words burst out and stopped her before she crossed the room. "My pal. Damn, Sydney, I couldn't..." The humiliation of it clawed at him again. "I could never get beyond that, and make you, well, a wife. It unmanned me. And I took it out on you."

"I thought you hated me."

He slapped the bottle back on the table. "It was easier to try to hate you than admit I couldn't arouse either one of us. That I was inadequate."

"But I was." Baffled, she took a step toward him. "I know I was useless to you in bed—before you told me, I knew it. And you had to go elsewhere for what I couldn't give you."

"I cheated on you," he said flatly. "I lied and cheated my closest friend. I hated the way you'd started to look at me, the way I started to look at myself. So I went out to prove my manhood elsewhere, and hurt you. When you found out, I did the manly thing and turned the blame on you. Hell, Sydney, we were barely speaking to each other by that time. Except in public."

"I know. And I remember how I reacted, the hateful things I said to you. I let pride cost me a friend."

"I lost a friend, too. I've never been sorrier for anything in my life." It cost him to walk to her, to take her hand. "You didn't ruin anything, Syd. At least not alone."

"I need a friend, Peter. I very badly need a friend."

He brushed a tear away with his thumb. "Willing to give me another shot?" Smiling a little, he took out his handkerchief. "Here. Blow your nose and sit down."

She did, clinging to his hand. "Was that the only reason it didn't work. Because we couldn't handle the bedroom?"

"That was a big one. Other than that, we're too much alike. It's too easy for us to step behind breeding and let a wound bleed us dry. Hell, Syd, what were we doing getting married?"

"Doing what everyone told us."

"There you go."

Comforted, she brought his hand to her cheek. "Are you happy, Peter?"

"I'm getting there. How about you? President Hayward."

She laughed. "Were you surprised?"

"Flabbergasted. I was so proud of you."

"Don't. You'll make me cry again."

"I've got a better idea." He kissed her forehead. "Come out in the kitchen. I'll fix us a sandwich and you can tell me what you've been up to besides big business."

It was almost easy. There was some awkwardness, little patches of caution, but the bond that had once held them together had stretched instead of broken. Slowly, carefully, they were easing the tension on it.

Over rye bread and coffee, she tried to tell him the rest. "Have you ever been in love, Peter?"

"Marsha Rosenbloom."

"That was when we were fourteen."

"And she'd already given up a training bra," he said with his mouth full. "I was deeply in love." Then he smiled at her. "No, I've escaped that particular madness."

"If you were, if you found yourself in love with someone, would you consider marriage again?"

"I don't know. I'd like to think I'd do a better job of it, but I don't know. Who is he?"

Stalling, she poured more coffee. "He's an artist. A carpenter."

"Which?"

"Both. He sculpts, and he builds. I've only known him a little while, just since June."

"Moving quick, Sydney?"

"I know. That's part of the problem. Everything moves fast with Mikhail. He's so bold and sure and full of emotion. Like his work, I suppose."

As two and two began to make four, his brows shot up. "The Russian?"

"Ukrainian," she corrected automatically.

"Good God, Stanislaski, right? There's a piece of his in the White House."

"Is there?" She gave Peter a bemused smile. "He didn't mention it. He took me home to meet his family, this wonderful family, but he didn't tell me his work's in the White House. It shows you where his priorities lie."

"And you're in love with him."

"Yes. He wants to marry me." She shook her head. "I got two proposals in the same night. One from Mikhail, and one from Channing Warfield."

"Lord, Sydney, not Channing. He's not your type."

She shoved the coffee aside to lean closer. "Why?"

"In the first place he's nearly humorless. He'd bore you mindless. The only thing he knows about Daddy's business is how to take clients to lunch. And his only true love is his tailor."

She really smiled. "I've missed you, Peter."

He took her hand again. "What about your big, bold artist?"

"He doesn't have a tailor, or take clients to lunch. And he makes me laugh. Peter, I couldn't bear to marry him and have it fall apart on me again."

"I can't tell you if it's right. And if I were you, I wouldn't listen to anyone's good-intentioned advice this time around."

"But you'll give me some anyway?"

"But I'll give you some anyway," he agreed, and felt years drop away. "Don't judge whatever you have with him by the mess we made. Just ask yourself a couple of questions. Does he make you happy? Do you trust him? How do you imagine your life with him? How do you imagine it without him?"

"And when I have the answers?"

"You'll know what to do." He kissed the hand joined with his. "I love you, Sydney."

"I love you, too."

Answer the questions, she thought as she pushed the elevator button in Mikhail's lobby. It was twenty-four hours since Peter had listed them, but she hadn't allowed herself to think of them. Hadn't had to, she corrected as she stepped inside the car. She already knew the answers.

Did he make her happy? Yes, wildly happy.

Did she trust him? Without reservation.

Her life with him? A roller coaster of emotions, demands, arguments, laughter, frustration.

Without him? Blank.

She simply couldn't imagine it. She would have her work, her routine, her ambitions. No, she'd never be without a purpose again. But without him, it would all be straight lines.

So she knew what to do. If it wasn't too late.

There was the scent of drywall dust in the hallway when she stepped out of the elevator. She glanced up to see the ceiling had been replaced, the seams taped, mudded and sanded. All that was left to be done here was the paint and trim.

He did good work, she thought, as she ran her hand along the wall. In a short amount of time, he'd taken a sad old building and turned it into something solid and good. There was still work ahead, weeks before the last nail would be hammered. But what he fixed would last.

Pressing a hand to her stomach, she knocked on his door. And hoped.

There wasn't a sound from inside. No blare of music, no click of work boots on wood. Surely he hadn't gone to bed, she told herself. It was barely ten. She knocked again, louder, and wondered if she should call out his name.

A door opened—not his, but the one just down the hall. Keely poked her head out. After one quick glance at Sydney, the friendliness washed out of her face.

"He's not here," she said. Her champagne voice had gone flat. Keely didn't know the details, but she was sure of one thing. This was the woman who had put Mikhail in a miserable mood for the past few days.

"Oh." Sydney's hand dropped to her side. "Do you know where he is?"

"Out." Keely struggled not to notice that there was misery in Sydney's eyes, as well.

"I see." Sydney willed her shoulders not to slump. "I'll just wait."

"Suit yourself," Keely said with a shrug. What did she care if the woman was obviously in love? This was the woman who'd hurt her pal. As an actress Keely prided herself on recognizing the mood beneath the actions. Mikhail might have been fiercely angry over the past few days, but beneath the short temper had been raw, seeping hurt. And she'd put it there. What did it matter if she was suffering, too?

Of course it mattered. Keely's sentimental heart went gooey in her chest.

"Listen, he'll probably be back soon. Do you want a drink or something?"

"No, really. I'm fine. How's, ah, your apartment coming?"

"New stove works like a champ." Unable to be anything but kind, Keely leaned on the jamb. "They've still got a little of this and that—especially with the damage those idiots did." She brightened. "Hey, did you know they arrested a guy?"

"Yes." Janine had told her about Lloyd's arrest when she'd called in. "I'm sorry. He was only trying to get back at me."

"It's not your fault the guy's a jerk. Anyway, they sucked up the water, and Mik mixed up some stuff to get the paint off the brick. They had to tear out the ceiling in the apartment below that empty place. And the floors buckled up pretty bad." She shrugged again. "You know, Mik, he'll fix it up."

Yes, she knew Mik. "Do you know if there was much damage to Mrs. Wolburg's things?"

"The rugs are a loss. A lot of other things were pretty soggy. They'll dry out." More comfortable, Keely took a bite of the banana she'd been holding behind her back. "Her grandson was by. She's doing real good. Using a walker and everything already, and crabbing about coming home. We're planning on throwing her a welcome-back party next month. Maybe you'd like to come.''

''I'd—'' They both turned at the whine of the elevator.

The doors opened, and deep voices raised in some robust Ukrainian folk song poured out just ahead of the two men. They were both a little drunk, more than a little grubby, and the way their arms were wrapped around each other, it was impossible to say who was supporting whom. Sydney noticed the blood first. It was smeared on Mikhail's white T-shirt, obviously from the cuts on his lip and over his eye.

''My God.''

The sound of her voice had Mikhail's head whipping up like a wolf. His grin faded to a surly stare as he and his brother stumbled to a halt.

''What do you want?'' The words were thickened with vodka and not at all welcoming.

''What happened to you?'' She was already rushing toward them. ''Was there an accident?''

''Hey, pretty lady.'' Alex smiled charmingly though his left eye was puffy with bruises and nearly swollen shut. ''We had a hell'va party. Should've been there. Right, bro?''

Mikhail responded by giving him a sluggish punch in the stomach. Sydney decided it was meant as affection as Mikhail then turned, locked his brother in a bear hug, kissed both his cheeks.

While Mikhail searched his pockets for keys, Sydney turned to Alex. ''What happened? Who did this to you?''

''Did what?'' He tried to wink at Keely and winced. ''Oh, this?'' He touched ginger fingers to his eye and grinned. "He's always had a sneaky left." He shot his brother a look of bleary admiration while Mikhail fought to fit what seemed like a very tiny key in an even tinier lock. "I got a couple good ones in under his guard. Wouldn't have caught him if he hadn't been drunk. Course I was drunk, too." He weaved toward Keely's door. "Hey, Keely, my beautiful gold-haired dream, got a raw steak?"

"No." But having sympathy for the stupid, she took his arm. "Come on, champ, I'll pour you into a cab."

"Let's go dancing," he suggested as she guided him back to the elevator. "Like to dance?"

"I live for it." She glanced over her shoulder as she shoved him into the elevator. "Good luck," she told Sydney.

She was going to need it, Sydney decided, as she walked up behind Mikhail just as he managed to open his own door. He shoved it back, nearly caught her in the nose, but her reflexes were better than his at the moment.

"You've been fighting with your brother," she accused.

"So?" He thought it was a shame, a damn shame, that the sight of her was sobering him up so quickly. "You would rather I fight with strangers?"

"Oh, sit down." Using her temporary advantage, she shoved him into a chair. She strode off into the bathroom, muttering to herself. When she came back with a wet washcloth and antiseptic, he was up again, leaning out the window, trying to clear his head.

"Are you sick?"

He pulled his head in and turned back, disdain clear on his battered face. "Stanislaskis don't get sick from vodka.'' Maybe a little queasy, he thought, when the vodka was followed by a couple of solid rights to the gut. Then he grinned. His baby brother had a hell of a punch.

''Just drunk then,'' she said primly, and pointed to the chair. ''Sit down. I'll clean your face.''

''I don't need nursing.'' But he sat, because it felt better that way.

''What you need is a keeper.'' Bending over, she began to dab at the cut above his eye while he tried to resist the urge to lay his cheek against the soft swell of her breast. ''Going out and getting drunk, beating up your brother. Why would you do such a stupid thing?''

He scowled at her. ''It felt good.''

''Oh, I'm sure it feels marvelous to have a naked fist popped in your eye.'' She tilted his head as she worked. That eye was going to bruise dramatically before morning. ''I can't imagine what your mother would say if she knew.''

''She would say nothing. She'd smack us both.'' His breath hissed when she slopped on the antiseptic. ''Even when he starts it she smacks us both.'' Indignation shimmered. ''Explain that.''

''I'm sure you both deserved it. Pathetic,'' she muttered, then looked down at his hands. ''Idiot!'' The skin on the knuckles was bruised and broken. ''You're an artist, damn it. You have no business hurting your hands.''

It felt good, incredibly good to have her touching and scolding him. Any minute he was going to pull her into his lap and beg.

"I do what I like with my own hands," he said. And thought about what he'd like to be doing with them right now.

"You do what you like, period," she tossed back as she gently cleaned his knuckles. "Shouting at people, punching people. Drinking until you smell like the inside of a vodka bottle."

He wasn't so drunk he didn't know an insult when he heard one. Nudging her aside, he stood and, staggering only a little, disappeared into the next room. A moment later, she heard the shower running.

This wasn't the way she'd planned it, Sydney thought, wringing the washcloth in her hands. She was supposed to come to him, tell him how much she loved him, ask him to forgive her for being a fool. And he was supposed to be kind and understanding, taking her in his arms, telling her she'd made him the happiest man in the world.

Instead he'd been drunk and surly. And she'd been snappish and critical.

Well, he deserved it. Before she had time to think, she'd heaved the washcloth toward the kitchen, where it slapped wetly against the wall then slid down to the sink. She stared at it for a minute, then down at her own hands.

She'd thrown something. And it felt wonderful. Glancing around, she spotted a paperback book and sent it sailing. A plastic cup gave a nice ring when it hit the wall, but she'd have preferred the crash of glass. Snatching up a battered sneaker, she prepared to heave that, as well. A sound in the doorway had her turning, redirecting aim and shooting it straight into Mikhail's damp, naked chest. His breath woofed out.

"What are you doing?"

"Throwing things." She snatched up the second shoe and let it fly. He caught that one before it beaned him.

"You leave me, go away without a word, and you come to throw things?"

"That's right."

Eyes narrowed, he tested the weight of the shoe he held. It was tempting, very tempting to see if he could land it on the point of that jutting chin. On an oath, he dropped it. However much she deserved it, he just couldn't hit a woman.

"Where did you go?"

She tossed her hair back. "I went to see Peter."

He shoved his bruised hands into the pockets of the jeans he'd tugged on. "You leave me to go see another man, then you come back to throw shoes at my head. Tell me why I shouldn't just toss you out that window and be done with it."

"It was important that I see him, that I talk to him. And I—"

"You hurt me," he blurted out. The words burned on his tongue. He hated to admit it. "Do you think I care about getting a punch in the face? You'd already twisted my heart. This I can fight," he said, touching the back of his hand to his cut lip. "What you do to me inside leaves me helpless. And I hate it."

"I'm sorry." She took a step toward him but saw she wasn't yet welcome. "I was afraid I'd hurt you more if I tried to give you what you wanted. Mikhail, listen, please. Peter was the only person who cared for me. For *me*. My parents..." She could only shake her head. "They're not like yours. They wanted what was best for me, I'm sure, but their way of giving it was to hire nannies and buy me pretty clothes, send me to the best boarding school. You don't know how lonely it was." Impatient, she rubbed her fingers over her eyes to dry them. "I only had Peter, and then I lost him. What I feel for you is so much bigger, so much more, that I don't know what I'd do if I lost you."

He was softening. She could do that to him, as well. No matter how he tried to harden his heart, she could melt it. "You left me, Sydney. I'm not lost."

"I had to see him. I hurt him terribly, Mikhail. I was convinced that I'd ruined the marriage, the friendship, the love. What if I'd done the same with us?" With a little sigh, she walked to the window. "The funny thing was, he was carrying around the same guilt, the same remorse, the same fears. Talking with him, being friends again, made all the difference."

"I'm not angry that you talked to him, but that you went away. I was afraid you wouldn't come back."

She turned from the window. "I'm finished with running. I only went away because I'd hoped I could come back to you. Really come back."

He stared into her eyes, trying to see inside. "Have you?"

"Yes." She let out a shaky breath. "All the answers are yes. We walked through this building once, and I could hear the voices, all the sounds behind the doors. The smells, the laughing. I envied you belonging here. I need to belong. I want to have the chance to belong. To have that family you said was inside us."

She reached up, drawing a chain from around her neck. At the end, the little ruby flashed its flame.

Shaken, he crossed the room to cup the ring in his hand. "You wear it," he murmured.

"I was afraid to keep it on my finger. That I'd lose it. I need you to tell me if you still want me to have it."

His eyes came back to hers and locked. Even as he touched his lips to hers gently, he watched her. "I didn't ask you right the first time."

"I didn't answer right the first time." She took his face in her hands to kiss him again, to feel again. "You were perfect."

"I was clumsy. Angry that the banker had asked you before me."

Eyes wet, she smiled. "What banker? I don't know any bankers."

Unfastening the chain from around her neck, he set it aside. "It was not how I'd planned it. There was no music."

"I hear music."

"No soft words, no pretty light, no flowers."

"There's a moon. I still have the first rose you gave me."

Touched, he kissed her hands. "I told you only what I wanted, not what I'd give. You have my heart, Sydney. As long as it beats. My life is your life." He slipped the ring onto her finger. "Will you belong to me?'

She curled her fingers to keep the ring in place. "I already do."

* * * * *

Look for more scintillating Stanislaski stories
from Nora Roberts
in Silhouette Special Edition

FOUR UNIQUE SERIES
FOR EVERY WOMAN YOU ARE...

Silhouette Romance®

Love, at its most tender, provocative,
emotional... in stories that will make you laugh and
cry while bringing you the magic of falling in love.

6 titles per month

Silhouette Special Edition®

Sophisticated, substantial and packed with
emotion, these powerful novels of life and love will
capture your imagination and steal your heart.

6 titles per month

SILHOUETTE *Desire*®

Open the door to romance and passion. Humorous,
emotional, compelling—yet always a believable
and sensuous story—Silhouette Desire never
fails to deliver on the promise of love.

6 titles per month

SILHOUETTE·INTIMATE·MOMENTS®

Enter a world of excitement, of romance
heightened by suspense, adventure and the
passions every woman dreams of. Let us
sweep you away.

4 titles per month